I0541054

MACLAREN STRONG

THE CLAN MACLAREN #5

NANCY PENNICK

MACLAREN STRONG
A CLAN MACLAREN NOVEL
Copyright © 2020 by Nancy Pennick

ISBN: 978-1-68046-875-5

Published by Satin Romance
An Imprint of Melange Books, LLC
White Bear Lake, MN 55110
www.satinromance.com

Names, characters, and incidents depicted in this book are products of the author's imagination or are used fictitiously. Any resemblance to actual events, locales, organizations, or persons, living or dead, is entirely coincidental and beyond the intent of the author or the publisher. No part of this book may be reproduced or transmitted in any form or by any means, electronic or mechanical, including photocopying, recording, or by any information storage and retrieval system, without permission in writing from the publisher except for the use of brief quotations in a book review or scholarly journal.

Published in the United States of America.

Cover Design by Caroline Andrus

For my cousin,
Elizabeth

CHAPTER 1

June 1728

*E*lizabeth MacLaren did not resemble anyone in the family. Her cornflower blue eyes which could melt the hardest of hearts and the shade of golden-copper hair were uniquely hers. She had natural curl, unlike the rest of the MacLarens, making her the envy of the family. At nine years of age, she'd already developed a strong personality and stood up for her convictions, yet all who met her, loved her, for she was kind and caring plus a loyal friend.

The moment the newborn was placed in Juliet's arms, she vowed to protect Lizbeth with her life. The tufts of orange on the baby's sweet head had reminded her of the great queen of England, Elizabeth, who also bore the same color. Juliet immediately knew it would be the child's name.

A portrait of her majesty, Queen Elizabeth, had hung in one of the long hallways at her family estate in England. As a young girl, Juliet would gaze at the painting in awe, amazed a woman had ruled the country for so long. Elizabeth's reign had been known as The Golden

Age, one of peace and prosperity, which mirrored the feeling Lizbeth had brought to the family's home in America.

Juliet sat in her rocking chair on the front porch enjoying the sun and children at play. Slowly over time, they'd settled into their life in Perth Amboy, New Jersey, and it began to feel like home just as her husband Ross had pledged. *Is it too good to be true? After all the turmoil in our first years of marriage, the next ten have been filled with peace.* Not every day had been a good one, but the most challenging were quickly resolved.

"Mummy! Alec will not stop chasing me," Lizbeth called to her.

Alec stopped short and placed his hands on his hips. "You are the one who wanted me to chase you." He glanced toward Juliet with a pleading look for help.

Her heart soared at the fine man Alec had become. He'd been five when they came to America, so innocent with his white blond hair and emerald eyes. Unable to pronounce all the syllables in Elizabeth's name, he'd been the one to christen her Lizbeth.

Her adopted son would turn sixteen in December, and she wondered if more physical changes were in store. His hair had slowly darkened over the years until it had reached light brown, yet he kept the MacLaren emerald eyes. Each day he reminded Juliet more and more of Ross even though he was the biological child of his deceased sister, Greer, and her husband, Ewan Kincaid. Ewan had been killed in the 1715 Uprising in Scotland and soon after Greer died of fever. Juliet shook her head as she recalled those unhappy times but reminded herself how lucky she had become.

Juliet gestured for the two children to come and sit on the porch steps. Lizbeth skipped toward her as Alec trailed behind dragging his feet.

"Lizbeth, Alec has just come home from school in Boston and is doing you a favor. After morning chores, he dedicates an hour to do as you wish, whether it be riding, reading or chasing you through the yard. He does not have to give you any time since he has become a man. Remember that."

Lizbeth stuck out her lower lip. "Why do my brothers have to be so much older than me? I like playing with them."

"There are many playmates in the village," Alec answered. "Why we even have our own school now, thanks to Uncle Brodie. You never had to ride in the wagon to Dame School in Amboy. It was a long, cold trek in the winter."

Lizbeth rolled her eyes. "That old story?"

Juliet laughed. "Your brother is right. Uncle Brodie's dream to start a new village on his land grew with you, Lizbeth. By the time you were ready for school, Gregor's Cove had a blacksmith, a chapel and a general store. He felt it was time for a school and inquired in town for a teacher to move here."

"I went to her house for Dame School until I was seven."

"Yes, you did. You learned your numbers and letters from Mrs. Murphy then graduated to the grammar school built in the village."

"I learned them on the horn book, right, Mummy?" Lizbeth pursed her lips. "I still have it in my room. I would like to share with someone who needs it."

"Very thoughtful, my darling."

"Auntie Heather was not fond of us attending school here in Gregor's Cove." Alec reminded Juliet. "I stopped going into town as much and did not see my cousins as often. When the snow got bad, I used to stay at her and Uncle Jamie's house for days during the winters. She misses those times together."

"Why doesn't Aunt Heather's family move to Gregor's Cove, Mummy?" Lizbeth widened her eyes as she looked at Juliet. "Da would have both sisters here, and Auntie would not be sad."

Juliet's heart melted. *Oh, my little dove. You always want to solve everyone's problems.* "You know why. Uncle Jamie owns the blacksmith shop in Perth Amboy. He needs to live close to his work."

"I would love to go to school with my cousins." Lizbeth crossed her arms. "Alec had all the fun."

"James and Annie were too young to go to school with me, Lizbeth. They are closer to your age. Rosslyn was the only cousin who attended, and she was two years younger. You did not miss out." Alec stood and tousled her hair. "Look, Cowan, is bringing your horse."

"Aye, sister, Princess Elizabeth is ready for yer morning ride." Cowan bowed.

Her eldest son had grown so fast, leaving his boyhood years too

3

quickly. Juliet had known Cowan since she'd first come to Glenhaven in Scotland to marry Ross. He had been a seven-year-old messenger boy from their village who delivered information to the chieftain of the clan, Ross' father, Laird Donnach MacLaren.

Cowan had turned twenty-one in the spring. A distant cousin to the MacLarens, he'd come to America with the family, mainly for his safety after rescuing Ross from an English prison. His mother begged Ross to take him to the colonies, relinquishing her parental rights.

Shorter than the other MacLarens, Cowan held his own with his quick wit, kindness and strength. He had handsome features and was growing a beard like his favorite uncle. His coloring was nothing special, a medium brown, unlike Brodie's auburn tones, but the facial hair suited him.

Cowan's eleventh birthday had taken place aboard the ship Pembroke, during their 1718 crossing to America. Once they were situated in Perth Amboy, Ross and Juliet deemed him too old to attend Dame School with Alec. Ross had inquired about education opportunities in Boston. Their friend, Hiram Coward, a government official in the city, offered to look after the boy while he attended university and now did the same for Alec. Juliet had worried Cowan might not hold his own against the other students, since she'd been the one to tutor him while in her care. Cowan assured her she had done her duty and proved to be an excellent pupil. Now graduated and back at their farm, Cowan still went to Boston to study, wanting to become a lawyer like Hiram.

Juliet tuned back into her children's conversation, listening to their speech. Each spoke in a different way, and although questioned by others through the years, she had stopped defending them long ago. People eventually accepted the family members as they were.

Cowan had kept his Scottish brogue, and Alec took up her English accent when he was barely four. Lizbeth spoke in what Juliet could only call American-speak, like her brother-in-law Brodie Gregor. Her daughter attended school and played with children from Scotland, England, Germany and Holland. The second generation seemed to blend seamlessly together picking up on each other's cadence and new words for things.

"I will take ye riding, sister," Cowan said. "Then yer coming home to help Mum with dinner."

"But it is summer, Cowan. I do not have to go to school, and Mummy will not mind if I wade in the stream for a bit." Lizbeth's lovely blue eyes landed on Juliet.

"You may be indulged today since school has ended," Juliet answered. "Starting tomorrow, you will have a list of chores to complete like your brothers."

Alec jumped from the steps, poked Lizbeth in the side and taunted, "You cannot get your way all the time, my pretty. We have to work for our supper." He took off running, letting out a wild hoot.

"Ooh!" Lizbeth hopped up and stamped her foot. "I will get you, Alec MacLaren. Just you wait!"

Juliet laughed as she watched Alec run down the road toward Gregor's Cove. He'd acquired many friends and was popular among his peers, but he was not going there to find them. "Be back in two hours!" she called after him as she felt a hand on her shoulder.

"He is going to the blacksmiths, aye?" Ross said. "I believe his sword is ready."

"Why does Alec need a sword, Da?" Lizbeth wrinkled her nose.

"Every Scot has one, my princess." Ross bowed his head. "To protect those he loves."

"Cowan?" Lizbeth turned to him. "Do you have one?"

"I do. Da and I practice in the woods where no one can get hurt or in the way."

"Oh." Lizbeth pursed her lips. "When do I get to make a sword?"

Ross threw his head back and laughed. "Who does that sound like, wife?"

Juliet smiled up at him. "Your sister, Glynis. She has trained her niece well."

"Auntie Glynis says women can do anything," Lizbeth answered. "Sometimes better than a man." She giggled.

"Yer auntie is right about many things, daughter," Ross said. "But, not that."

Lizbeth stopped laughing. "I think she would say those are fighting words, Da."

5

"Oh, no!" Ross clapped his forehead. "Do not tell her then."

Lizbeth laughed. "I will not, but only if one day you will let me design my own sword."

Ross nodded at Cowan standing between two horses. "It looks like yer brother is ready to take ye for a ride." He took Juliet's hand. "And, I need to speak with yer mother."

"About the sword?" Lizbeth's eyes widened in delight.

"No, nothing of the sort. Go now, before I change my mind and put ye to work."

Lizbeth ran to Cowan who swung her up into the saddle. Juliet joined Ross at the edge of the steps and watched the two riders and horses trot down the path to the woods. Ross slipped his arm around her waist, pulling Juliet toward him and nuzzled her neck. "I thought they wouldna ever leave."

"Ross, whatever do you have in mind?" Juliet looked at him, batting her lashes.

"'Tis hard to find time for us, Juliet. I love my children, but they always seem to be underfoot." He glanced over his shoulder. "I dinna see a one of them. I would love to carry ye up the stairs to our bedroom if ye are in agreement."

"I think I am." Juliet wrapped her arms around him, taking in his fresh outdoor scent mixed with a light sweat from morning chores. She ran her hand along his clean-shaven jaw and up into his dark hair which fell around his shoulders. "After thirteen years of marriage, I am happy you still want me so."

"Never speak in such a manner," Ross whispered into her hair. "I will always want ye, no matter how old ye are. Besides, ye still look young, wife. A bonny lass at two and thirty."

"You have given us a happy life, Ross." Juliet held out her hands. "We lived on Brodie's farm barely a year before you bought this land and built our house. You, in turn, helped him fulfill his dream of Gregor's Cove. Many Scots who arrived in America had resigned themselves to servitude. Instead, they met Broden Gregor on the docks of Boston Harbor, looking for those who had a skill to offer or the will to work. He brought them here and gave them a place to live. All he asked was for a year of free labor in return. Once their debt was paid, they could follow their lot in life. Everyone stays. We help each other here and do not need slaves to tend our crops or take care of our homes." She looked away. "As some others have done."

"Do not think of him today, Juliet. 'Tis the beginning of summer, we have our children home, and I have my morning chores done. So, I will ask again. Will ye join me?"

"Yes," she whispered, taking his hand and stepping into their two-story colonial home.

The house was not a Scottish castle or an English manor as Ross reminded her. Juliet did not need a grand lifestyle as she told him many times and loved the home more than any place she had lived. Family had helped build and decorate each room, and every piece of furniture had a story. Some had been ordered from the Vogel's general store in Perth Amboy while others had been lovingly made by Ross' strong hands. Besides his job as Amboy's blacksmith, his sister Heather's husband, Jamie, was also good at carpentry and lent an extra hand.

The couple crept up the steps. When Ross got to the top, he turned to Juliet. "This is our house. Why are we acting like robbers in the middle of the night?"

Juliet laughed and fell into his arms. "Because we feel as if we are." She walked to the end of the hallway and into their bedroom.

A breeze flowed through the open windows, and the muslin curtains fluttered in the air currents. Juliet rolled the rose and blue quilt Heather had made them down to the edge of the bed and smoothed the sheets. She felt Ross' hands on her back, untying her laces and unbraiding her hair.

"I love ye, Juliet, and the color of yer hair. 'Twas the first thing I noticed when I met ye, standing so tall and proud in the grand dining hall of my father's castle. The candlelight gave yer brown hair a soft red glow, and I wished to run my hands through the silky locks. I moved from there to yer sweet lips, the color of a pink rose, plump and ready to be kissed. Then," Ross said and turned her toward him as her dress floated to the floor, "I drank ye into my soul." His lips came down softly on hers, and Juliet's heart flipped as it always did. Her love for him was as strong as his and passion never waned.

They sank to the bed as one, and Juliet was carried away to another place where she and Ross only existed and shared their love.

---

*R*oss felt a warm hand on his back, massaging the muscles. "A little higher, please."

"So, you are awake," Juliet said.

"Aye, I am enjoying the quiet." Juliet's fingers circled the scar on his shoulder. "Is it quite faded, wife? After all the years, it should be."

"I will always see it, Ross, even if it is a faint scar or completely gone. I will never forgive John Alder for trying to kill you and driving us from our home."

"But, the knife didna kill me. The duke had poor aim." Ross chuckled and jumped as Juliet poked his side. He slid out from under her hand and sat up on the mattress. "I never thought we'd escape the man, Juliet. His obsession with ye must have waned when we left Scotland since we have lived here in peace for years."

"From the letters we receive from your parents, brother Duncan, and his wife, it appears John gave up building Essex Manor of Scotland soon after we left."

"What did Alder think he was doing, Juliet? He planned to build a manor in Scotland when he had land to oversee in England. God's teeth! He is the Duke of Essex. I still question if the man is daft or cunning."

"John wanted to torment us, and the only way he could was to be in close proximity. If you remember, he threatened me and said the manor would be my new home. I shudder every time I think of it. I cannot believe I was once in love with the man."

"Ye didna ken, my love. John thought he'd found an impressionable young girl who'd love and obey him because one day he'd be Duke of Essex."

"He was kind and charming when he visited my father's home, Ross. John planned to ask for my hand in marriage the day the proclamation arrived."

"Good thing it did," Ross snarled. "Yer father sold ye to the highest bidder and John lost."

"It sounds terrible when you put it that way. Father is a weak man. He's apologized for offering me as collateral to the king to pay his debt and I forgave him. How can I not, when it sent me to you?"

"Then we agree. Life is as it should be. John Alder is no longer a threat to you or our family."

"When John left Scotland, it was a sign, Ross. He admitted defeat and went home to England the same year we sailed to America."

"I can only hope 'tis true."

"It took years to believe, but I do now." Juliet rubbed Ross' arm. "I am glad you finally trust Hiram and Edward." She pursed her lips. "It took a long time."

"The Coward brothers are Englishmen, Juliet, born and bred into the aristocracy. Edward is an officer in the King's army and a loyal friend to John Alder, and Hiram is an official in the colonial government who could have me arrested at a moment's notice. Forgive me if it took some time to trust them."

"Those Sassenachs. How could they be trusted?" Juliet teased as she shook her head. "I almost miss your father calling me the name."

Ross gathered her in his arms and kissed the side of her head, breathing in her warm vanilla scent. "I can call ye Sassenach any time ye wish," he whispered and nuzzled against her naked body.

"I do not miss it that much." Juliet laughed, making Ross' heart soar. He loved to see Juliet happy and enjoying life.

When they first met, Ross never dreamed they would sail on a ship to America to start a new life. In fact, if someone told him his sister Heather would already live in New Jersey by the time his family left Scotland, he would have laughed them out of the castle. His youngest sister, Heather had married Jamie MacGregor at age sixteen, and after the Uprising of '15, the MacGregor clan was in more danger than the rest. Donnach decided they must leave the country for their safety. Though frightened of being a pregnant wife in a foreign place, Heather still chose to leave with her husband.

And Glynis? His older sister by a year, his sibling soul mate, had volunteered to go with the young couple to the colonies. Strong and brave, Ross never pictured her falling in love with the captain of the Pembroke, Aaron Redding. Her story was full of pitfalls and hope, losing Aaron and finding him again to marry and sail away on his ship. Ross reconnected with his sister on his voyage to America which had turned tragic for his sister once again.

Barely a day from Boston Harbor, Aaron Redding had been lost to the sea during a violent storm. Devastated over losing him twice, Ross worried Glynis would not recover. Luckily, her first time in Perth Amboy had been a good one. Broden Gregor had befriended then fallen in love with his sister. He'd brought Glynis back to the living by hunting and fishing with her, offering to build her a small home on his land. He'd come close to asking her to marry him, and would have, if Aaron had not miraculously returned from the dead.

The second time, Aaron had not been as lucky. He truly died in the Atlantic Ocean ten years ago. Ross had watched the poor man drown after saving Glynis from the same fate. *Poor bastard. 'Tis the life of a sea captain, I guess. But I have Brodie to thank for helping Glynis live again. If he'd not been a drunken sot in prison when we arrived, my sister may never have found herself. She dedicated her days to nursing him back to health.*

"Ross? What are you thinking about?" Juliet slid her hand along his cheek.

"Glynis and Aaron."

"Oh."

"What do ye mean, wife?"

"Aaron has been dead a long while. I am surprised you are thinking of him and your sister as a couple."

"No, 'tis not what I am doing. Brodie is a fine man and a good husband to Glynis. I was thinking back to the days when we lived in Scotland and our lives since then. Did ye ever think we'd come to America?"

"Now I see. You are reliving our journey." Juliet turned to face him. "I never thought I would leave England, Ross, let alone Scotland. One thing I learned during our marriage is we can do anything as long as we are together."

"Aye, wife, where ye are is my home."

"And you, Ross, *are* my home."

CHAPTER 2

"*M*um! Da!" Alec's voice could be heard from the second floor.

Juliet looked at Ross and giggled. "We need to get dressed and quickly." She scrambled off the bed, picked up her clothes from the floor and threw her shift and green linen day dress over her head.

Ross struggled with his brown breeches after slipping on his faded red linen shirt. He glanced over at her and smiled. "I love ye."

"I love you, too. I will go see why Alec is anxious to see us. Take your time." When Juliet got to the top of the stairs, she called, "Alec?"

"Here. Sitting in the parlor, Mum. I did not think you were home."

Juliet glided down the stairs and around the banister to find Alec holding a letter in his hands. "Oh! I must call your father at once."

"He is here?" Alec lifted his brow.

"Yes, resting after his chores," Juliet answered. "Ross! Come quickly."

"Did Alec get his sword? I canna wait to see it." Ross pounded down the steps. "Son?"

"No, Da, it is still at Angus' shop."

"How is Angus doing? Or should I ask how his wife Nell and the bairn are doing?"

11

"The baby has grown fat since I last saw him." Alec laughed. "And still has no hair."

"It is common for some babies to have no hair, Alec," Juliet answered. "Little Angus will soon choose between his father's brown coloring or mother's red."

Angus Forbes had sailed on the same ship to America as Heather, Jamie and Glynis. He'd planned to be an indentured servant once they landed but Jamie had immediately recognized him as one of his clan, the MacGregors. He insisted Angus come to Perth Amboy to be his apprentice at the blacksmith shop. Since both sailed under assumed names, they kept their friendship a secret. To this day, no one knew they were MacGregors, except the adults of the MacLaren extended family. Jamie made a vow to his wife's father, Donnach MacLaren, he would keep Heather safe and would not go back on his word, never to use his real surname again.

Juliet recalled the times she and Ross had discussed the MacGregor predicament. The clan had a history for causing trouble, stealing, and taking what wasn't theirs. At one point, they'd even been stripped of their clan name by the king. Although the Indemnity Act of 1717 pardoned those who partook in the '15 rising, releasing them from jail or allowing clans to relocate, the whole clan of MacGregor had been excluded.

MacGregors may not be safe in England or Scotland, but in the colonies, people were more tolerant. In fact, Brodie's family was part of the MacGregor clan, known in the colonies as the Gregors. So many years had passed since the Jacobite Uprising, Juliet wondered if it would be safe for Heather's family to go home to Scotland. Yet, her life had roots in New Jersey. All her children were born in Perth Amboy.

"To this day, Juliet, we never know if someone is looking for Jamie," Ross had once told her. "More so than Angus. Jamie is tied to me through marriage, and if John Alder had his way, we'd both be hung from the neck for treason. He must remain a Mercer."

"Treason," Juliet remembered letting out a puff of air and crossing her arms. "Something John never proved for either of you."

"He'd find a way if we still lived at Glenhaven." Ross had scoffed. "We are better off living in America and keeping our secrets."

"Juliet? Did ye hear me?" Ross called to her, startling her back to the present. "I want to ken what the letter says. When we finish, we will send Alec to his aunties, so they can read it, too."

Juliet blinked and looked at Ross. "What? Yes, of course."

"Come and sit." Ross patted the settee with room for two.

"We must go to the village and visit the Forbes' baby," Juliet said as she sat. "Angus and Nell waited so long for a son after three girls. He was born six months ago, and we have only seen him three or four times."

"Aye, ye are right, wife." Ross slung his arm across the back of the small sofa and rubbed her back. "I visit Angus often for business and shoeing the horses, but ye arena always with me. When ye are, ye think of Nell and the bairn. The lassies play behind the forge where Angus can keep an eye on them, so I see them more often."

"We will remedy it soon." Juliet looked at Alec. "Would you like to read the letter to us?"

"May I?" Alec's eyes brightened.

"Who is it from?" Juliet asked.

Alec flipped through the pages to the end. "Auntie Eva."

"Wonderful!" Juliet's heart soared when she heard the name.

Eva had traveled to Scotland as her personal maid, but they were much more than nobility and servant. The girls had grown up together and were fast friends. Small but mighty, Eva was loyal to the core. Juliet could picture her standing with hands on hips, dark blond braid swinging in defiance as her blue-gray eyes pierced through her victim or whoever wronged them. When they arrived at Glenhaven Castle, Ross' younger brother, Duncan, and Eva fell in love. They married and had five children. Juliet regretted she wasn't present for the last baby's birth, a boy, three years ago.

Alec cleared his throat. "Greetings to all. I am writing this in time to be delivered to one of the early ships sailing to America from Crail. Uncle Gillanders has been so helpful in making sure our letters find their way on board any ship crossing the ocean during the season. Good thing he lives by the sea."

"What is the date she wrote the letter, lad?" Ross asked.

"April of this year, Da. Just a few months ago. Uncle Gill must have gotten this on the very first ship leaving port."

"Aye, he would. Gill is a verra kind man."

"The opposite of Grandda," Alec answered.

"Alec!" Amazed Alec still remembered his time at Glenhaven Castle, Juliet sometimes wished he did not have such a good memory. She tried to speak of Donnach as a loving grandfather, but the boy would stare at her as if she was the one with poor recall.

As chieftain of Clan MacLaren, Juliet tried to explain Donnach had the burden of taking care of the family and the people of the village. She explained the chieftain must be feared by his people and surrounding clans and Donnach's gruff exterior helped him rule well. For all he'd done to her, she understood the reasons for his actions.

Alec would counter his grandfather could still be kind to the family and did not have to shout commands. Everything had to be his way, and Juliet found it hard to disagree. She'd come to a shaky truce with Donnach before they left, knowing he never was fond of her. The man sold her out once and probably would do so again.

"Should I continue?" Alec asked.

"Yes, please." Juliet straightened her skirt although it did not need it.

"People are happy to see the sun and feel its warmth after the long winter. The gentle breezes once again have returned in place of the harsh winter ones. The village has come alive preparing for Beltane, vowing to have the biggest bonfire yet to celebrate the coming of the summer season. I have to admit I never get used to seeing people jump through the flames." Alec looked up, eyes wide. "I remember wanting to try!"

"No!" Juliet sat forward. "It is not safe, Alec."

"I will not, Mum. Besides, the fire we build here is so small I could jump over it and not get hurt." He chuckled as he returned to the letter and wiggled his eyebrows. "Ready for the update on the Essex Castle of Scotland?"

"Yes!" Juliet knew most of the details but loved to hear the latest on its demise.

When John Alder arrived in Scotland the fall of 1716, the MacLarens did not believe he would stay. He'd inherited his family estate after the death of his father and took the title of Duke of Essex. "He will tire of this folly," Donnach had said. Yet, he continued to stay at Fort Augustus and began to build a manor. His obsession with Juliet grew stronger, and John continued to find ways to upset their lives at Glenhaven Castle. He could never accept she chose Ross over him and refused to give up on ending her marriage any way he could.

The manor John commissioned was meant to be a place he and Juliet would eventually live. Reports of the abandoned dwelling had filled the MacLaren letters over the years. The family enjoyed the fact that John had lied about how the home was almost completed. When Ross was imprisoned, he'd told them the manor was far from finished, just a shell no higher than the first floor. Work had suddenly stopped when Ross and Juliet disappeared. Scavengers would sneak into the building site at night, helping themselves to rock, stone and tools, furthering its decay.

A year after Ross and Juliet set sail for America, Duncan, had decided to ride to Fort Augustus to see if the rumors were true and John had left Scotland. The family felt enough time had passed and deemed it safe to visit. He'd discovered John had gone to England for the summer after Ross and Juliet disappeared and had sent word to the fort he'd stay through the winter never to return., The work stoppage was real. Not one more brick or stone had been laid.

"The shell of the manor is almost overgrown with grass and weeds. A tree has sprouted up in the middle where the reception hall might have been." Alec laughed. "I would love a tree in our house."

"Perhaps when we build ye one, ye can find a good tree to be part of yer home," Ross replied.

"Da, you are too serious." Alec stared at him. "I am making a joke."

"And so am I, son." Ross smiled. "See? I do have a sense of humor."

"Ross." Juliet nudged her husband. "Let Alec read the letter. You two can banter later about the house Alec will live in some day with a tree sticking out of the top."

"Aye, lad, yer mother's right. Please, go on." Ross chuckled.

Alec needed a minute to contain his laughter then began to read. "Auntie lists the family members and gives a report on each one. She speaks of my cousin Julie first, who turned twelve this spring. Auntie says she is still quiet and reserved but will stand up for herself and others when she feels someone is wronged. Julie dotes on Grandda and always tries to cheer him up when he is in a foul mood." Alec paused. "Which is most of the time."

"Did she really say most of the time?" Juliet asked.

"No." Alec shook his head. "I added the last part."

"Alec!" Ross yelled. "Enough about your grandda."

"Sorry." Alec hung his head. "I can see her in my mind."

"Who, Alec?" Juliet asked.

"Your namesake, Mum, my cousin Juliet or known as Julie. She was dark-haired and blue-eyed, a pretty, gentle lass."

"She was." Juliet bobbed her head. "We only know about the others through letters and sketches. Does Eva say how they are faring?

"From what Auntie Eva says in the letter, the boys are doing well."

"'Tis good to hear," Ross announced with a nod of his head.

"Maybe not, Da." Alec stared at his parents. "Auntie Eva says she is sorry for changing the tone of her letter but feels we need to know of the distressing occurrences at Glenhaven. Little Greer has not been well."

Juliet looked at Ross. "The child has been weak since she was a baby, catching cold after cold and not growing as fast as her twin brother. He sat up months before she did, and Greer did not walk until she was past two. Oh, the poor little girl, what is wrong?"

"Greer keeps having fevers. They come and go." Alec answered.

"No!" Ross stood up, and Juliet slipped her hand in his.

"Like my mum in heaven," Alec said with a sad look on his face. "She never got better and died." He let out a breath. "But, Logan, her twin, is doing well. He follows his big brother Edward everywhere. Soon, they will both go away to school in France. Would I have gone with them, Da?"

"Aye, son, ye would have already been there."

"Auntie Eva ends her letter by saying Granny is sad and tired but will not leave Greer's side. She thinks Granny feels guilty and is trying to make amends from when her Greer died. Granny did not believe she was that sick and insisted Greer would get better."

"What does she say about Donnach?" Juliet asked.

"He is in fine health but locks himself away in his receiving room all day. He used to play with the children, come out for supper and kiss them goodnight. Now, he stays in the room conducting business, hardly eating and drinking whiskey." Alec glanced up at them. "It does not sound like a happy place."

"No," Ross said, shaking his head. "It doesna. This is the first we have heard of trying times. All the letters have been full of details of their busy daily lives. Antidotes. Greetings from villagers. If Eva felt she must write this, it must be bad." He jumped up and pounded a fist into the palm of his hand. "And, there is nothing I can do about it!"

"Da," Alec said. "I am sorry, but there is more."

"What can it be? Little Greer keeps falling ill, and my da has locked himself away to drink till he dies."

"There is no more bad news, just sadness. Auntie Eva ends by saying she feels all the MacLarens who live in America are bonding more and more each day while she and Duncan are lost and lonely. Besides our family, we live with others who came from Scotland and it appears we have our own clan here. She says she has no right to complain, but they miss us. Uncle Duncan alone has to shoulder the burdens of Glenhaven with your mother and father."

"We are MacLaren strong, wherever we live!" Ross paced the room. "And Glenhaven is not a burden. 'Tis our home, Alec. Dinna ever forget it."

"Ross, calm yourself." Juliet rose from the settee to head to the kitchen. "I am going to start dinner. Lizbeth and Cowan will soon be back and hungry."

"I will wait on the porch for them, Mum. I am sure they will want to read the letter."

"After we eat, ye will go across the way to yer Auntie Glynis' and let her see it," Ross called after him. He took Juliet by the arm and pulled her to him. "Och, Juliet. How much should we worry?"

"I do not know, Ross. But, Eva is a sensitive girl and loyal to a fault.

We are here, and she is not. It must break her heart. And," Juliet stared up into his bright green eyes. "She may be envious of our life. We send news of good crops, new homes, healthy children and babies coming into the family. America was not a place any of us wanted to live, but things have turned out well for us."

"Thanks mostly to Brodie."

Juliet gave him a little push. "You would have built me a house next to Heather's or bought land out here and began to farm. You were never idle, Ross. I had faith in you. Look what you gave the family. This wonderful house and a bountiful life."

"After what we went through to get here, I am glad ye kept yer faith." Ross lowered his head until their foreheads touched. "I canna do this without ye by my side. Ye ken that, wife."

"You could have done it without me, Ross, and if something ever happens to me, you will carry on. We have three children in our care."

"Cowan is not a child, Juliet. You need to stop thinking of him as such." Ross teased and placed a kiss on her lips.

"Have we done right by him, Ross?"

"Aye, lass, we did the best we could. Cowan writes letters to his mum once a month and bundles them to be sent to Scotland when the ships are sailing. He finished school at the top of his class and is studying to become a lawyer."

"When you list his accomplishments, it sounds good. Still, I wondered if we did right by him long ago when we forbade him to see Gwen."

"'Twas the right thing to do at the time. We decided we couldna stay friends with her mother after she married the bloody pig, Jasper Sexton, part of England's newly rich gentry and moved to his manor." He threw a hand in the air.

Juliet shivered. "Every time I hear his name…"

"'Tis why I dinna speak it, my love." Ross kissed her cheek.

"Come into the kitchen while I prepare dinner. We rarely have time to speak alone, and I want to continue this." Juliet tugged on his hand.

Ross sat at the kitchen table and said, "I will only stay if ye let me help."

"Here. Peel and cut these potatoes. Then you will not have idle hands."

"Ye ken what they say about idle hands."

"Are the devil's tools?" Juliet closed one eye. "Then you never have to worry about the devil chasing after you, Ross MacLaren."

Ross laughed and accepted the knife and potatoes from her. "I ken ye dinna like to hear news from the Sexton Estate, so I keep it from ye, Juliet. Whenever ye want, I will tell ye what I ken."

"Here is what I know." Juliet tended the fire and placed a pot of water over it. "Cowan met Gwen on the Pembroke. She was a lovely girl and his first love. We took that from him."

"Aye, Gwen is lovely on the inside, but a plain-looking lass compared to her mother."

"Ross!" Juliet faced him and gave him a look of disappointment. "I know you feel Cowan should marry the most beautiful woman in the world, but his heart still belongs to the girl he met on the ship ten years ago despite the fact we kept them apart."

"With good reason, Juliet. We agreed." Ross waved the cutting knife in the air. "Her mother became intoxicated by the Sexton wealth. On the ship Sophie was a widow with a child planning to become an indentured servant when she arrived. Instead her angelic face and blond locks caught Jasper's eye. It didna hurt she was connected to us, making her more appealing to the pig. He then concocted the story she was related to the chieftain of her clan, elevating her position so he could look as if he'd made a good match. Och! They deserve each other with their airs and ways."

Juliet slid into a seat across from Ross. "All right, tell me what you have heard."

CHAPTER 3

"Jasper Sexton is planning an extravagant party for his tenth wedding anniversary in August," Ross said. "Talk in town is it will be the biggest party Perth Amboy has ever seen."

"Biggest?" Juliet wrinkled her nose. "Amboy does not have many residents. Is Jasper planning to transport people to the manor?"

"He may invite people from New York and other places he does business. His da will come from England or may already be here to visit his grandchildren."

"Sophie has given Jasper two sons. I can picture him strutting like a rooster in front of his father boosting he produced Sexton heirs. Glynis told me Jasper was the only male in his generation. Now, he has provided two for the next. Word has it poor Gwen is in charge of the boys and their education." Juliet shook her head.

"Besides Sexton's two, she also teaches Ewan Buchanan."

"I did not know! Why did you not tell me the good news? Jasper lets one of his indentured servant's children come into his home and be educated? I might have to change my opinion of the man. Do you think he has a school for the others?"

"No." Ross smirked. "Norris Buchanan doesna consider himself a servant, although I believe he has five years left on his contract. He negotiated terms with Sexton when he first arrived for rights beyond his position. I have to say the man is not afraid to speak his mind."

"We do not know for certain, Ross."

"Och, I do. I have heard many stories and came to my own conclusion. Norris agreed to do Sexton's dirty work when he became his slave master. Jasper remains the benevolent proprietor…or so he believes."

"Sadly, from our time on the ship and what we learned about Norris, I think it could be true. Oh, Ross, it is the reason we did not want Cowan anywhere near the manor, and I have no desire to go there now or ever."

"We dinna have to go to the party, Juliet."

"It is months away, so I will not think of it yet. Besides, we may not be invited."

Ross frowned. "The man always invites us, but we politely turn down every invitation. Jasper will insist we come to this one."

"He cannot make us come, Ross."

Ross chuckled. "No, he canna, but ye ken what I mean. What would be our excuse when every person in town will be there and 'tis two months until the party?"

"True. But going to the manor will dredge up many memories, most of them not good."

Ross reached across the table and took her hand. "Some are good."

Juliet stared at her husband who tried to soothe her soul. "I did feel better after we spoke with May at Jasper and Sophie's wedding."

Juliet had met May Buchanan, Norris' wife, on the Pembroke during the crossing. They'd become friends, and their boys played each day. She had no idea May was the same woman, Mary MacDonald, who Ross was to wed before King George's proclamation came to be. The English monarch and Laird Donnach MacLaren had agreed to a marriage between a noblewoman and his son. Through a strange twist of fate, the English subject chosen to wed Ross had been Juliet.

May and Juliet had met daily on the ship, clueless of their connection. They'd never seen each other's husbands until a fight broke out between Norris and Ross on the top deck. Juliet could tell

May was still in love with Ross, and she suspected Norris thought so, too.

Norris drank heavily on the ship and continued to imbibe once in America. When he was under the influence, he'd say their child, Ewan, wasn't his but Ross'. He accused May of sleeping with Ross well past their breakup, and Juliet almost believed it until May had confirmed otherwise at the Sexton wedding. She hadn't seen Ross since the autumn of 1714. Too much time had passed for the child to be his.

That day in the Sexton barn, Ross had offered May to leave Norris and come live at Brodie's farm. She'd said she could not keep her son from his father, plus another baby was on the way, reminding Juliet she had told her of the pregnancy while on the ship. They said their goodbyes, and Juliet felt she'd never see her friend again.

"Juliet? Are ye all right?"

"Just thinking." She lifted a shoulder. "We tried to save May but ended up helping her sister instead."

"Aye, we did. Nell and Angus have had a peaceful life in Amboy and now here in Gregor's Cove."

"I do not know how peaceful it can be with four children under the age of nine," Juliet said with a laugh.

"Verra true." Ross chuckled. "We did a good thing, Juliet."

Juliet closed her eyes. The conversation she had with May's sister, Nell, during the same wedding came to mind as clear as if it happened yesterday.

After the ceremony, a ruckus had disturbed everyone's dinner. Norris had gotten word his sister-in-law planned to leave the estate with Angus Forbes, and he was going to stop her.

Nell had blinked at Juliet from across the table, looking so much like May. Her blue eyes held a look of fright and her ginger hair fell around her face in the afternoon heat as she asked, *"Did I do something wrong?"*

"No, you did not. Let me ask you one question. Do you love Angus? Really love him? Because I will not let the men fight for you if you do not."

Nell's eyes welled with tears. "Angus is a kind and decent man with good morals. How could I not love him?"

Juliet shot daggers at the woman. "Answer the question." She knew if they left

Nell behind, Angus would be devastated. He already had one fiancée leave him, but it was best for it to happen now.

"*I will learn to love him,*" *Nell whispered.* "*Please, Juliet, let me come with ye. I will always be a servant here.*"

"*You will treat him well?*"

"*Aye.*"

Juliet had kept the conversation private, never telling Ross about Nell's feelings. She'd hoped the girl would grow to love Angus, who was a wonderful man, and perhaps she had. Tall and gangly with a beak nose and long face, his outward appearance was average at best. But, Angus' heart made up for any shortcomings. Everyone in the village loved him.

"Aye, things have worked out well for us all, Juliet," Ross said, breaking into her thoughts.

"Except Cowan," Juliet reminded him. "We have to let him choose his way, Ross. We cannot forbid him to see anyone or dictate his life anymore."

"I had hoped he'd meet someone in Boston." Ross rubbed his face.

"He was too busy studying and helping Hiram with his sickly wife."

"May she rest in peace." Ross crossed himself. "I never understood why Hiram married the poor lass in the first place, Juliet. Her health was already suspect."

"For love?"

Ross stared at her. "The man who loves my sister with his whole heart to this verra day?" He shook his head. "No."

"He wanted someone to take care of as he wished to do for Glynis," Juliet answered. "Penelope was a kind, sweet woman, and he had six good years with her."

"Penelope knew he was a good match and would take care of her after her ailing father passed."

"Ross!" Juliet glared at him. "Do not speak ill of the dead." She paused. "Besides, I am running out of good things to say about her."

Ross threw back his head and laughed. "Then you agree? I thought Glynis would scratch Penelope's eyes out at the wedding when she swooned and almost fainted after the ceremony. Hiram caught her in time, and Glynis grumbled she was putting on quite the show."

"Oh, Ross!" Juliet giggled and placed her hand on her chest. "You never told me."

"Aye, Glynis felt Penelope only married Hiram for position and money. Her brother inherited the father's estate, and the two bairns never got along. He probably would have had her removed from the home after the earl passed. We also felt she wasna sick, feigning illness after illness until the winter fever really took her."

"I felt sorry for her, Ross, and never truly believed her stories. Whenever we saw her, Penelope looked perfectly fine to me. Perhaps she had to pretend she was ill to gain attention. Sadly, the fever did take her life in the end. Hiram has just come out of mourning, and we need to be supportive. I hope he will visit more now that he does not have to tend to Penelope's needs."

"She used illness as an excuse to keep Hiram in Boston," Ross said. "The woman always had a look on her face as if she smelled something foul when they arrived for a visit."

Juliet held back from laughing and tapped her husband on the shoulder. "Ross, you need to stop. I have a feeling you and Glynis have had many conversations about Hiram and Penelope."

"Oh, we have. Glynis thinks they never…"

"Mummy! Da! We're home." Lizbeth's voice rang through the house. "Where are you?"

"In here, my little dove," Juliet answered.

The girl stood in the kitchen doorway, cheeks flushed pink, her golden-copper hair in a tumble of wild curls. "I have to tell you something before Cowan comes inside. He is on the porch with Alec reading Auntie Eva's letter now."

"Whatever could it be?" Ross turned to face her and patted the bench next to him. "Come and sit by yer da."

"I promised I would not tell, but you have to know." Lizbeth studied her hands after she sat. "When Cowan and I go riding, he meets Gwen by the pond."

"How long has this been going on?" Ross asked.

"Since he came home from Boston. Today they kissed. They thought I did not see, but I did." Lizbeth let out a breath. "I did not mind the meetings. I thought it romantic. Kissing?" She crossed her arms. "I cannot stay quiet any longer."

"You did the right thing." Ross put his arm around her and squeezed. "Cowan shouldna put ye in such a position and never told ye to keep it a secret."

"Do you think they will marry, Da?" Lizbeth looked up at him with such a sweet expression, it melted Juliet's heart.

"I dinna ken, lass."

"Lizbeth," Juliet said. "Gwen and Cowan have known each other for a long time, since he was ten and she eleven."

"Yes, I know the story. Gwen is a year older than Cowan. She almost did not speak to him on the ship because she considered him a young child." Lizbeth laughed. "But, he won her over. Once you landed, you lived with Auntie Heather. Gwen and her mother were invited to stay, too. But," Lizbeth said, wiggling her fingers and changing her voice to sound like a scary witch. "The evil Jasper Sexton swept Sophie along with her daughter, Gwen, away to his dark castle in the country, never to be seen again."

"Oh, Lizbeth." Juliet laughed. "You *do* have an imagination."

"My teacher says the same thing." Lizbeth grinned.

"Well, my bonny one," Ross said and patted her back. "You ken why we stay away from the estate."

"The people there are not kind and think only of themselves," Lizbeth repeated what she'd been told since birth. "But, not Gwen, Da. She is sweet and very kind to me."

"Aye, she is." Ross nodded. "'Tis the other people at the manor."

"Why not let Cowan rescue Gwen from the evil castle, Da? The story would have a happy ending."

Ross stared at Juliet, and she hoped he remembered her words. It was time to let Cowan make his own decisions. "We have kept them apart, yet they keep finding their way back to each other. 'Tis a sign, Juliet?"

"I think so."

Cowan rushed into the kitchen, out of breath. "Has she told ye?" He scratched the top of his head in thought, ready to tell his side if she had.

"Aye, son, Lizbeth has told us ye meet Gwen in the woods. Ye are a grown man, and we canna stop ye from seeing her," Ross answered. "If ye wish, ye may court her. We would prefer ye bring her here. Do not make visits to Sexton Estates."

"I will have to call on her at the at the manor some of the time." Cowan's face brightened. "Am I allowed to fetch her for a visit, Da? 'Tis not proper to ask her to ride here alone."

"Ye may take the wagon or ride there and escort her back. But I am afraid I have to agree with ye, ye'll have to go there occasionally." Ross turned to his daughter. "Lizbeth, would ye tell Alec dinner is ready?"

Lizbeth skipped from the room, and Ross slid from the bench. "I only ask ye to protect the family, Cowan. Dinna let Sexton charm ye with his wealth."

"Da, our family comes first. I have kent Jasper Sexton since I was a young lad and am aware of the things he has done."

"He may not like you taking away the boys' tutor, Cowan," Juliet said.

"It will not be a problem, Mum. Jasper has sent for an English professor to come and live at the manor. He is to arrive in September. Gwen will no longer teach the boys."

"She is their main caregiver, and they may not give her up so easily," Juliet replied with a smirk. "I never thought Sophie could turn into the shrew she is today. When we met her she was sweet and caring yet determined to find her own way even if it meant being an indentured servant."

"Jasper dotes on her, Mum." Cowan balled his hands into fists. "But, not Gwen. She will deny he strikes her, but I ken he does."

"We will do our best to welcome her," Juliet said. "You say you love her still?"

"Aye, Mum, since the day I met her on the Pembroke."

"It is not a boy's adoration, a love which may wane over time?"

"No, I want to marry her."

"Does she want to marry ye?" Ross looked up at him.

"Aye, she does." Cowan nodded eagerly. "I would like to build a home in Gregor's Cove if only…" His voice drifted away.

"If only what, lad?"

"If only I didna want to be a lawyer. To be a good one, I should live in Boston. I want to go there. Hiram said he would help me find a job and lodging."

"Ye have spoken to Hiram?"

Juliet saw the hurt in Ross' eyes. "Of course, Ross. Cowan lived with Hiram during his schooling, and Hiram is considered part of our family." She looked at Cowan. "I am proud of you, and I am sure Gracie is, too. Have you written to your mother of your plans?"

"I will." Cowan stared at the floor. "I have been busy since I returned from Boston."

"Cowan," Juliet said as she got up from the table and walked to him. "You deserve happiness. Ever since you were a young boy, you took on everyone's problems or did their bidding. Now, it is your time."

"Do you think so, Mum?" Cowan lifted his head and met her eyes.

"I know so." Juliet kissed him on the cheek. "Now, sit. I need to tend to our food."

Lizbeth and Alec came laughing into the kitchen and took their seats.

"Mum, Alec has promised to take me to see his sword once he has done his chores. I cannot wait to see it!" Lizbeth's eyes shone. "Afterward, when I get home, I will start a sketch of mine."

Alec looked at Juliet and smiled. "Auntie Glynis will love to hear *that* story." He glanced over at Ross. "Right, Da?"

"Pass the potatoes," Ross grunted.

Juliet stifled a laugh. Ross was a good father, but when it came to girls, he stumbled blindly along. He'd turned to her many times, asking if he did or said the right thing to Lizbeth. He could hunt and fish with the boys, teach them carpentry and sword-fighting. Those skills came easy. He had a special bond with both boys, knowing Alec as his nephew from birth then swearing to protect him as his father at the age of three.

Cowan had always been a visitor to the castle, a favorite of Donnach's. The boy was good at spying, reporting news and relaying messages. Cowan and Alec became fast friends despite the five-year age difference. After Cowan risked his life to save Ross when he was imprisoned at Fort Augustus, they knew he would not be safe in Scotland. If John Alder got word the boy had anything to do with the escape, he'd have no trouble arresting him. Ross and Cowan were bonded ever since.

"What were the two of ye laughing about?" Cowan asked.

"Nothing." Lizbeth played with her food.

Cowan gave Alec a hard stare. "She told ye."

"Then do not kiss girls in front of her." Alec teased.

"Och! Does everyone have to ken my business?" Cowan scooped more potatoes onto his plate.

"It is hard not to," Alec said with a laugh. He looked around the table for agreement.

Finally, Cowan broke into a smile. "I will miss this family when I am married."

"We will miss you, too," Juliet said, trying her best to hide her feelings.

"Now we have finished, I must get back to work," Ross said. "Thank ye for the wonderful meal, wife."

"I admit I have gotten better at cooking over the years with all the help I received." Juliet got up and joined Ross at the back door. "Thank you for earlier," she whispered.

"My pleasure," Ross said with a kiss to her cheek then left to complete his chores.

CHAPTER 4

"Glynis MacLaren Redding Gregor," Glynis yelled. "How many times do I have to remember to use flour to thicken the sauce? Och! I could stand here all day and wonder why I have broth instead of a cream sauce for dinner. I will never be a cook or one who wants to wile the day away mending and sewing."

"Are you speaking to yourself again, wife?" Brodie gathered Glynis into his arms and kissed her neck. "We have many people in Gregor's Cove who can help with those chores."

"No." Glynis shook her head. "I must learn." She turned in his arms and looked into his brown eyes which reminded her of whiskey. "But, I am better at this." Glynis stood on her tiptoes to kiss Brodie's mouth.

"Do not start or I will never go out the door." Brodie brushed his lips across her forehead. "Do you ever get enough?" He leaned back and smiled.

"Of ye? No," she whispered.

"Mum, Da!"

Pounding footsteps alerted Glynis the boys had dressed and were ready for the day.

"Da promised to take us hunting," Rory said, placing his hands on his hips and looking so like his father. "Just us lads."

Glynis feigned shock and hurt by rolling her head and putting her hand over her heart. "Without me?"

"Aye, Mum, but…" Rory ran to her and threw his arms around her waist. "I did not mean to hurt your feelings."

"Ye dinna, Rory, I was teasing ye." Glynis ran her hand through his auburn hair, straightening the messy locks. "Did ye wash when ye woke?"

"I will just get dirty again!" Rory gave her such a look of indignation she had to laugh.

"True, but ye still need to wash. Go to the bucket in the corner and do it there."

Glynis threw him the towel draped over her shoulder and watched her second born stroll to the bucket and tentatively stick the tips of his fingers into the water. He would turn eight soon, and she'd have to stop thinking of him as her baby.

"I, on the other hand, mother dear, am washed and ready."

Glynis turned to her eldest son. "Aye, Aaron, ye are." Her heart swelled with pride as the boy walked toward her. Brown hair, blue-eyed like his father, Aaron Redding, he'd already caught the attention of many girls. He'd soon be ten years old, ready to go to school in Boston, and Glynis did not know how she could let him go.

Hiram Coward, her long-time friend, planned an extended visit this summer, and they'd discuss the boys' education. She'd missed Hiram over the last six years since he married the sickly Penelope. "A wonderful actress, if I may say," she said under her breath.

"What did you say?" Aaron wrinkled his brow.

"Nothing."

"Oh, talking to yourself again."

"Will you stop!" Glynis giggled. "Yer da told me the same thing before you two ruffians came down the stairs."

"No more teasing your mother, lads," Brodie said, rubbing Glynis' arms. "Eat your porridge, and we will be on our way."

"May I have coffee today, Mum?" Rory asked from the corner of the kitchen.

"Oh, aye, ye may." Glynis nodded.

Brodie gave her a questioning look. "The lad likes coffee?"

"Watch and learn." Glynis pulled Brodie with her. She took a mug, filled it with milk and a splash of coffee.

"I see." Brodie brought her to him. "You never stop surprising me with your skills."

Glynis toyed with the front of his shirt. "Ye will miss me on the hunt."

"I promised the lads." Brodie dropped his voice. "You are not really angry?"

"No, I have things to do." Glynis raised a shoulder. "You never ken, I might go into town. I may see Jasper Sexton and invite him for tea."

Brodie let out a hearty laugh. "I might have to stay home after all."

"No!" Came from both boys.

"Then bring me a bowl of porridge so we can leave as the sun rises." Brodie gazed down at Glynis. "I thank you for our boys."

"They are strong and healthy ones, eh?"

"Different, yet I see you in each one."

"Do ye? Rory reminds me of ye."

"In looks, but stubbornness?" Brodie nodded toward the boy who patted his cheeks with wet fingertips.

Glynis wrapped her arms around her husband's waist. "Wait till he can grow a beard. It will drag on the ground as he walks, and Rory will say, 'Why should I trim it? It will only grow again.'"

Her mind suddenly flashed back to a time when Brodie had given up on life. He'd let his hair and beard grow, did not wash and drank each day away. *Because of me. I left him for Aaron.*

Glynis had come to Perth Amboy with her youngest sister, Heather, and her husband Jamie. Pregnant with their first child, Heather was only sixteen. Their parents feared for her safety, and Glynis volunteered to leave her life in Scotland, cross the Atlantic and settle in a new land to protect her sister. She had no time for men, preferring to hunt, fish and sword fight with any willing man. Also, she left no loved one behind except family.

"And Aaron?" Brodie broke into her thoughts. "May look like his da…"

31

"But takes after you." Glynis poked him. "Capable and dependable...with a good sense of humor. The first Aaron?" She closed one eye. "Definitely capable and dependable but verra serious."

The couple chuckled and sat at the table with the boys. Aaron had filled bowls with porridge for everyone. "My father, Aaron Redding..."

Glynis smiled inwardly whenever the boy spoke of his father. He'd always start his question or statement the same way he did now.

"Could he hunt, Mum?"

"I never asked if he could. We wintered in London and bought our food. He could fish, and we did many times from the Pembroke deck." *We fished from the same ocean which took yer da's life.* For a moment, a feeling of melancholy swept through Glynis. She fought the tears stinging her eyes and reflected back on the times spent on the high seas.

On the Pembroke, Glynis had met three men, one who would become her husband, another a dear friend, and the last an adversary. She had not gone looking for romance, but when she laid eyes on the captain of the ship, Glynis fell instantly in love. Aaron Redding was dashing in his uniform and out of it, too. She wanted to sail the world with him, go on adventures she could never imagine. They had two good years together after he returned from a terrible hurricane at sea. Everyone in Amboy convinced her he was dead and to go on with her life, but Aaron did not perish. The minute he laid his brilliant blue eyes on her again, she knew she would be his forever.

Glynis had met Brodie her first time in Amboy. He'd befriended her, invited her to the farm to live life her way. Hunting in his woods, they got to know each other. He told her he loved her yet did not push. Brodie gave her space and time to heal from Aaron's supposed death. Glynis had come to the decision she could grow to love him and begin life again when Aaron appeared as if through magic or witchcraft. She wed Aaron within days and left, never knowing Brodie planned to ask her to marry him.

Two years later, on her return trip to Perth Amboy, Glynis found Brodie in a jail cell. His father, a magistrate for the town, had had his fill of Brodie's drunken ways and hoped some time in prison would bring him to his senses. Once he saw his plan did not work, Jock had Brodie sign for a tour of duty with the English army. Glynis used everything in her power to stop the enlistment, saying Brodie was not in his right mind when he signed the contract. Hiram had come to the rescue, representing Brodie as his lawyer. If not for Hiram, Glynis knew Brodie would have been under Edward Coward's command in New York until this day.

Glynis had nursed Brodie back to health, and when he discovered she was pregnant with Aaron's child, he proposed marriage. He swore he'd be a good father, offering to claim the baby as his own. Glynis could never agree to the deception. She would never let her son or daughter forget their father, the man who died rescuing them from the ocean. "Aaron or Erin will ken their father. Aye, they will have yer last name, Brodie, but we will tell him or her of Aaron Redding," she had told him.

Glynis felt a kiss on the cheek.

"We are leaving, love. Do you need anything before I leave?"

"No," Glynis answered. "I am fine. Lads?" She held out her arms, and each boy dropped into one to receive a kiss on the top of their heads. "Dinna cause yer da any grief. Do as he says."

"We will." Rory waved his hand as he followed the others out the door.

Glynis got up and wandered about the house. It appeared in order, so she grabbed her mending basket and sat on the front porch. Across the way and down the road a half mile, her brother Ross had built a house. Brodie sold fifty acres of land to him, cut right into the middle of his own holdings. She protested, saying his dream would not be fulfilled if he sold off land.

Brodie had smiled, took her in his arms and said, "Thank you for caring, but you see, this is my dream."

She couldn't have loved him more than at that moment. Gregor's Cove became a reality after Ross built his house, stables and barn. More services were needed and going into town could take much of the day. They needed help in their small village which was growing at a rapid pace. Most of the people who settled in the Cove had come off the ships, ones who planned to be indentured servants. Surprised by Brodie's offer to come to Gregor's Cove, they grabbed the chance to be part of a new village.

"Auntie Glynis!"

She looked up at the sound of the familiar voice. "Alec! Good day to ye. If ye came to see the lads, they are hunting with Brodie."

"No, Da sent me to see you." Alec waved his hand in the air.

"What do ye have there?" Glynis sat forward, trying to see.

"A letter. From Auntie Eva."

"Get up here then and let me read it." Glynis sat back in thought. "Have ye eaten dinner?"

"Aye, then I was to come here."

"I have been out here that long and could be burning mine?" Glynis hopped from the chair, not realizing how much time had passed. "I will be right back." She could hear Alec chuckling as she raced to the kitchen. "Och, bloody hell."

The pot had boiled over and onto the fire, and she grabbed a tong to swing the arm which held the pot out and away from the flame. A quick stir, she let it sit as it was. "Dinna worry. They will eat anything after being in the woods most of the day."

Glynis returned to the porch. "Now, let me see the letter. Ye have read it, aye?"

"Everyone at my house has heard or read it. After you finish, I am to take it to Auntie Heather."

"Why so quickly? We have shared letters before without such urgency." Glynis noticed the grim look on Alec's face. "Oh." She took the paper from his outstretched hand and ran her hand over the now-cracked seal. "Da," she whispered. "Your crest. How I miss ye so."

"I do not." Alec stood in front of her, arms crossed.

"Ye still hold a grudge against the old man?" Glynis closed one eye as she looked up from the letter. "'Tis not a good thing to do, nephew. The resentment will grow in yer belly until ye have a sour taste in yer mouth all the time. Ye are too young to keep those feelings in yer heart. Time to let them go."

"I cannot."

"Stubborn, like all the MacLarens. I will give ye that." Glynis shook her head and settled in to read. When finished, she noticed Alec had not moved. "Eva always sends glad tidings. Glenhaven must be in dire need of help if she wrote this. Ten years ago, I would have been on the first ship sailing to England or Scotland. Now, my life there seems like a dream. So much time has passed. So much changed."

"I would never go back." Alec stomped his foot. "This is my home. My da owns land I will inherit one day. I will live here forever."

"Formidable words, Alec. Ye sound like me. I would have said the same about Glenhaven." Glynis held out her arms. "Now, look at me."

"I would not want to leave you." Alec ran to her open arms, and she wrapped them around him.

"'Tis a hard thing to do, Alec. When I left my family, it felt as if someone ripped my heart from my chest. But, time heals. Besides, ye arena going anywhere, are ye?"

Her brother, Ross, may have spoken about a return, and Alec became concerned. She made a note to visit him once Alec left for Heather's.

"No, I do not think so. Mum is happy here, Auntie. She is never afraid as she was in Scotland."

"I canna believe ye remember yer time there. When ye left ye were only a lad of five."

"Mum and Da say I have a good memory. It is why I do well at school."

"Ah, school." Glynis decided to change the subject. "Hiram will arrive in a few days."

"How long will he stay?"

"I hope for the summer. Most in the city who can afford it, escaped the summer heat and disease which comes with it."

"Is that what killed Penelope?"

Glynis lifted a shoulder. "We dinna ken, lad. She died in the month of March and believe winter fever 'twas the cause. If she would have listened to Hiram and accompanied him on his visits more often, she may have not contracted the disease. The sun and fresh air would have helped her grow stronger. She may have fought off the illness if she wasna skin and bone."

"Penelope always said a lady eats a few bits of food and should be satisfied."

Glynis laughed until she had to hold her belly to catch her breath. "Did she now? Dinna believe a word she told ye, nephew. Women

deserve to eat as much as they wish. Never judge a lassie on her looks."
She pointed at him. "Do ye hear me?"

"Oh, aye, I do. You would chase me with yer broom if I thought
otherwise." Alec chuckled.

"I have more than a broom." Glynis winked.

"Oh! Which reminds me. I have something to tell you. My sword is
ready. Angus said he'd put on the finishing touches and I can retrieve it
tomorrow."

"Did ye have the MacLaren crest embedded in the handle?"

"And a place for the emerald. An early gift from Da for my
sixteenth birthday."

"Which is in December so quite the early present."

"Angus measured the emerald and said he'd forge a spot for it. I am
to keep it with me until then. He did not want his girls to find it and
think it was a bauble for them. When I go to the shop, we will put it in
together."

"Angus is a thoughtful man. He could have taken the emerald and
done it himself. Instead, he wanted ye to be part of the ceremony.
Sometimes 'tis the small things which matter most. Remember that,
Alec."

"I will." He nodded with a solemn look on his face.

Her heart skipped a beat as she recognized her sister Greer in his
serious face. She'd been the practical one of the family, watching over
her younger siblings with the greatest of care. Alec inherited her
green eyes along with the shape of her lovely face and lips. Glynis
wondered if the will of the MacLaren's was strong enough to make
his hair darker than it already was. The white blond of his childhood
had slowly faded to a light brown. With or without their dark hair, he
was a handsome lad. Soon he'd be aware of how much, when the
girls of Boston set their eyes on him after he returned for fall
semester.

"I cannot wait to show Hiram my sword," Alec said.

"He may have to borrow mine and have a one-on-one duel with ye
when he arrives."

"I hope so. I want the duke to see I have become a man."

"Oh, so now Uncle Hiram is a duke, eh?"

"He will be one day, Auntie. It is the reason Penelope married him."

"Och, laddie! Dinna say that."

"No, Auntie. I heard her speaking in the parlor with her fancy friends. She did not know I was still home, thinking Uncle and I had left for the day."

"Why did you not tell me?" Glynis crushed the letter in her hand.

"Careful." Alec waved a hand. "I have to deliver the note to Auntie Heather."

"Answer the question, lad."

"They had already been married three years." Alec shrugged. "What could be done? I see fire in your eyes now, Auntie. Imagine if I told you then."

"Hiram did not deserve to be treated so by that witch!" Glynis crossed herself. "May she rest in peace."

"If it helps, I think Uncle liked being married. He would always smile when he introduced Penelope as his wife. She was a good companion and held wonderful parties at the house, even inviting the British general."

"Brodie and I were never invited to one of those wonderful gatherings." Glynis made a face which made Alec laugh.

"I love you, Aunt Glynis. You speak your mind and are loyal to a fault. Now, if you would return the letter to my possession, I will be on my way."

"Tell Heather we must speak, the three of us including Ross."

"I will."

Alec bounded down the porch steps and strode to his mount tied to a post at the entrance to the front yard. He placed his foot in the stirrup then let it slip back to the ground. "Do you hear someone yelling, Auntie?"

Glynis rose from her seat and joined him in time to see a man galloping in their direction, road dust flying in all directions. She shaded her eyes with a hand to get a better look. "Is that Keith O'Neill?"

Keith had crossed the Atlantic with Glynis and became one of the people Brodie invited to Perth Amboy along with Murray and Bridget

Drummond who lived a mile down the road. He was an expert fisherman and carpenter, skills needed in the town. Keith decided to work with Brodie's father, Jock, for a few years running his fishing fleet. When Brodie began to expand the village, Keith decided to come to Gregor's Cove and help people build homes, shops and furniture. In his late twenties when he arrived, he'd remained unmarried until he met a widow with an eight-year-old son in Gregor's Cove. Together they had a daughter, and the children helped them run a thriving business from their home.

"He is yelling something, Auntie," Alec said. "I cannot make out what he says."

Keith pulled up on the reins when he reached them. "Thank the Lord in heaven, yer here, Glynis. There's an emergency in the village. The forge is on fire."

CHAPTER 5

*G*lynis turned to Alec. "Run to the back of the house and into the woods. Call for yer uncle. Ye have hunted with them before, ye ken where they go. Do not stop until ye find them. Once ye do, ride home and tell yer da." She looked at Keith. "I dinna have time to ready my horse, can ye take me?"

Keith extended his hand and pulled Glynis up behind him. "I organized the fire brigade before I came. A chain of men with buckets is already formed and working to put it out."

"Good." Glynis was glad Brodie insisted on safety and had ordered leather buckets to be stored for firefighting. Men had volunteered to be part of the fire brigade with Keith acting as chief. "Was anyone in the forge?"

"Aye, we believe Angus was."

"No!" Glynis jabbed him in the back. "Hurry, Keith!"

---

*T*hey had two rabbits, a squirrel and not much else, but Brodie enjoyed spending time with his sons. The years had gone too quickly, and he couldn't believe Aaron would leave with Hiram

Coward to attend school in Boston with Rory not far behind. *But then I will have more time with my bonny wife.*

Brodie smiled as he thought of the first time he'd seen Glynis. Raven hair, flying in all directions, walking down the gangway of the Pembroke with her family. Dressed in blue silk, she planned to marry the captain of the ship later in the day. When her emerald eyes met his, he knew no one would ever tell her what to do. He'd wished he'd gotten the privilege of meeting her first, never wanting to tame her spirit. His heart beat faster every time she came near and still did to this day.

"Well, lads, we should head for home. Mum probably has burned dinner while she waited for us."

"She always burns dinner, Da," Rory said, looking up at him with a smile.

Brodie tousled his son's hair. "Do not let her hear you say so."

Aaron caught up to them. "Rory, did you hear anything in the woods today?"

Brodie wrinkled his brow. "What do you mean, son? There are always noises in the forest. Animals, birds…"

"No." Aaron shook his head. "Strange noises."

Brodie gave the boy a scolding look. "Do not try to scare your brother, Aaron."

"I am not." Aaron lifted his chin, reminding him of Glynis.

"He is right, Da. We have heard footsteps like someone followed us." Rory defended his brother and stamped his feet on the ground to demonstrate.

"Could be someone from the Cove out for a hunt. These woods belong to everyone in the village now."

"Would they not show themselves?" Aaron asked.

Brodie had to agree the boy was right. "Aye, they would."

Rory tugged on his father's shirt, eyes wide. "We told you! Listen! I hear screaming."

"What?" Brodie tuned in to the sounds of the forest. He heard the crackling of twigs and the crunch of dried leaves. Someone was coming their way at a quick pace. His rifle had been set back in its casing, and he reached for it now. "Get behind me," he whispered.

Once in place, the trio stood perfectly still, straining to pick up the sound.

"There it is again." Aaron held up a finger. "Coming from that direction." He pointed toward home.

"Hello! Anyone out here!" a voice shouted.

"It sounds like cousin Alec." Rory scrunched his face. "Alec?" he yelled.

"Aye! Where are you?"

Brodie looked at the boys. "Run to meet him. I fear something is wrong." He jogged behind his sons toward the spot where Alec stood.

Alec, out of breath and panting, placed his hands on his thighs. "Praise the Lord, I found you. Aunt Glynis sent me to find you."

Alarmed, Brodie asked, "Is she all right?"

"Aye, she is fine. Keith rode in from the village while I was at your house. The forge is on fire."

"Go!" Brodie yelled. He pushed the backs of his sons to move faster.

Alec jogged next to his uncle. "Auntie told me to go home and get my da after I found you."

"Lads," Brodie said to his sons. "You will run to the Drummonds and tell Murray. Stay with Bridget until we come for you."

The four burst from the woods, heading in different directions. Brodie ran to the barn and saddled his horse as he prayed the fire had been easily extinguished. He knew Glynis would be in the middle of the action, helping any way she could. "Go, Sir Prince!" He nudged the horse into a gallop.

Before he even reached Gregor's Cove, Brodie smelled the burning rubble and observed gray clouds of smoke rise in the air from the direction of the village. His heart tore in two, knowing the fire was larger than he hoped. When the village came into view, it appeared the brigade had contained the fire to the blacksmith shop which still burned. Screams and shouting came from all directions as he dismounted and took his horse far from the noise and fire. The last bit of flames licked at the blackened wood of what was left of the forge. He ran toward the madness, calling Glynis' name.

"Here, Brodie!" Glynis pushed through a crowd and rushed into his arms. "Angus was in the forge. He dinna get out. We are trying to find his body." She looked at him, tears filling her eyes. "But, 'tis not all. Two of his lassies were playing behind the shop. We havena been able to get back there yet. Nell is beside herself. She called Sarah home to help her with the bairn. Eve and Deborah stayed out to play."

"I will look for them." Brodie took her soot-stained face in his hands and kissed her lips. "Stay here."

"No! I will go with you."

"Now is not the time to be stubborn, wife." Brodie realized he fought a losing battle. "All right come with me. If I tell you to turn back, you will do as I say."

"Aye, husband." Glynis grabbed her top lip by her bottom teeth as if deciding to argue her case. "Och, we are wasting time. Hurry!"

Keith O'Neill saw Brodie and Glynis coming toward the forge, left his post and jogged over to them. "Brodie!" He rubbed his face, spreading the black soot across it. "Angus is gone. We know he was in the forge." A tear spilled from the corner of his eye.

"I am going to look for the lassies." Brodie patted Keith's arm. "You keep the men going until the fire is out."

"Head around the back way," Keith gestured with his hand. "'Tis the safest route."

The forge had been positioned at the end of the street, far enough away from the other shops in case of fire. The Forbes' home was only a quarter mile down the road, making it easy for Nell to come and get her daughters when needed. The girls preferred playing behind the shop, getting to visit customers, receiving coins to run to the general store for a sweet treat. When Angus had time, he'd make them trinkets from leftover pieces of metal or when he had downtime would carve them a toy.

Brodie and Glynis ran to the end of the street and around to the back of the shop. Gray smoke hung in the air clouding their vision, but Brodie could see what he thought were two little ragdolls lying in the grass. "Protect your face," Brodie shouted to Glynis. "From the smoke."

Glynis had already ripped a section of her skirt and tied a bandana around her nose. She tore a second and handed it to Brodie. As they grew closer, it appeared the older sister, Eve, had wrapped her arms around Deborah for protection and now lay on top of her. Glynis rushed to where the girls lay and fell to her knees. She rolled them onto their backs, their little faces blackened from the smoke and soot. "No!" She pounded on Deborah's chest then placed her ear to the child's mouth.

Brodie dropped down besides Glynis and did the same to Eve. The smoke had overpowered the little girls' lungs. He knew there was no hope but let Glynis try. Her sobs were more than he could bear yet he continued, matching her pushes to the chest and listening for breathing. "Glynis." He glanced at her.

"I ken." Glynis scooted next to Eve, checked for breathing, then slipped her hands under the girl's lifeless body and stood. "Take her, Brodie," she whispered. She bent down for the younger child she'd worked so hard to save and pulled her into her arms.

Without another word, Glynis and Brodie walked side by side through the smoke out to the street. When they appeared, people gasped, and one woman screamed. Brodie did not have to look. He recognized Nell's voice.

---

*A*s soon as Alec arrived home, Juliet knew something was wrong.

"Mum! Fire in the village," he called from outside.

Juliet rushed through the house and out to the barn. Alec knew where to find Ross, and she'd get the horses ready. Within minutes, Ross rushed into the barn.

"It's the blacksmith shop, Juliet." He swung up and over the saddle in one swift movement.

"Angus?" she asked as she widened her eyes in horror.

"Aye. He was inside working. I told Alec to stay with Lizbeth and not to come to the village. God knows where Cowan is."

The horses were familiar with the way to the village, and Juliet was grateful her mare did not need much guidance. Her heart was in her throat, and she could barely think. When they arrived at the village,

Nell stood at the edge of the road, baby Angus in her arms, Sarah at her side. Tears streamed down her face, and the little girl clutched her mother's side.

Ross helped Juliet from her horse. "I'll take care of our horses. I ken ye want to go to Nell."

"Thank you." Juliet rushed to where Nell stood. "May I hold him?" she offered.

"No." Nell shook her head. "I need him with me."

"Is there any word of Angus?"

"No one needs to tell me." Nell looked at Juliet through teary eyes. "He was in there." She hung her head. "Eve and Deborah were in the back."

Juliet took in a breath. "Oh! I am sorry."

Just as Ross joined them, shadowy figures could be seen coming through the smoke giving Juliet an eerie chill. As they emerged into clearer air, she saw Brodie and Glynis carrying two little girls, heads fallen back, arms dangling at their sides. Nell screamed, and Juliet reached for the baby as Nell dropped to the ground, sobbing.

Juliet met Ross' eyes and shook her head, not knowing what to say. Her heart broke for Nell's loss and for all the people of Gregor's Cove who knew and loved Angus.

It rained the day of the funeral, changing to a light drizzle as people began to congregate in front of the chapel. The women wore dark clothes and bonnets covering their heads. The men were dressed in their Sunday best. The minister from St. Peter's Episcopal Church in Perth Amboy would hold a service. Brodie had designated an area behind the church as a cemetery, and Angus with his daughters would become part of the small number of people already buried there.

Nell insisted Eve and Deborah share Angus' casket. Keith O'Neill created a beautiful remembrance which brought tears to every person who gazed upon it. He'd carved a cherubic angel on the top of the closed casket where each girl lay on either side of their father. The angel of protection, Archangel Michael, had been cut into the lid above Angus, running the full length of the casket.

The villagers had helped set tables around the Forbes' yard and brought food and drink for after the service. Nell thanked them for their help but insisted she could manage.

Many people from Perth Amboy, who also knew Angus, arrived for the ceremony along with Ross' sister and family. He found them outside the church, Heather leaning against her husband, Jamie.

"Och, Ross, dinna be jealous but Angus was like a brother to me," Heather said in a teary voice.

"I wouldna be angry or jealous, Heather." Ross rubbed her arm and looked at Jamie. "Ye have lost a brother, too. One of yer clan."

"Aye." Jamie swiped at a tear trying to escape his eye. "He always said one day he'd sail back to Crail and visit his mum and da. Angus was so proud of his wife and bairns, he wanted them to meet his family. And now…?" He dropped his head.

"I have spoken to Nell," Heather said. "She appears to have lost her mind, Ross. We must speak with her after Angus and his bairns are laid to rest."

"Lost her mind?" Ross wrinkled his brow.

"I will tell ye when we are all together." Heather nodded toward Juliet. "Poor sister has her hands full with my brood."

"They are good bairns," Ross answered. "She is getting them ready to head into the chapel. Let us join her."

Rosslyn, Heather's oldest at eleven, Annie aged ten and Lizbeth held hands as they walked to the entrance. The girls were the best of friends, and the only females, besides Julie and Greer in Scotland, of the next generation. Glynis and Brodie caught up with the group, and Ross smiled as he watched his sister straighten her boys' shirts and slick back their hair. Heather's son, James, ran up to his cousin Rory to join the procession into the chapel.

Each family filled a row, Ross with Juliet, their grown sons and Lizbeth. He leaned to Juliet and whispered, "Heather thinks something is wrong with Nell."

"She is grieving, Ross. Heather needs to leave the poor woman alone," Juliet whispered back.

"Ah, but then 'twould not be my sister." Ross lifted a brow, the MacLaren brow as Juliet liked to call it. His mother had always done so, and her children took up the habit.

Juliet smiled. "No, it would not."

The service ended, and the pall bearers were called to the front. Ross joined Jamie, Cowan, Alec and other friends of Angus' to carry the man and his girls to their final resting place. Sobs could be heard throughout the chapel as they lifted the coffin to their shoulders. It became eerily quiet as they exited the building. Even the animals of the forest reacted to the sad day and made no noise.

Women from the village gathered around Nell and her children, helping and guiding them from the church to the cemetery and back to the Forbes' home. Ross watched her carefully for any signs of madness but saw none. Nell walked along expressionless, never responding to condolences.

The drizzle had finally ended, and the sun fought to push through the gray clouds. People mingled in the Forbes' yard, and children played farther in the back. At the cemetery Ross had said a silent Gaelic prayer for Angus and honored him by using his given surname, MacGregor. He looked at Nell holding baby Angus and hoped one day he could tell the lad his father's real story.

Heather interrupted his thoughts by pulling him by the arm. "We need to speak over there." She bobbed her head to where her husband, Juliet, Glynis and Brodie stood.

"About?"

"For one, the letter. I didna get to read it as soon as you and Glynis did." Heather came to a stop when she reached the others. "What shall we do about the family in Scotland? Da would never lock himself away without good reason."

"There is a good excuse," Glynis answered. "Da needs to do something. He canna help little Greer, so he helps our clan. 'Tis why he locks himself away in the receiving room," She paused with a sigh. "He drinks to forget what is outside his door."

"A good thought, sister. Ye ken him well," Ross said.

"Well, what are we to do?" Heather stared at them. "We canna go there."

Jamie shook his head. "'Tis my fault we canna go."

"Dinna ever say that, husband," Heather answered. "No one is at fault. We need to find a way to help."

"This may help," Glynis said. "The Pembroke is due into port soon and should be arriving in Perth Amboy within a week. Noah always stops on his way down the coast to visit me and bring us gifts from his adventures. There might be more letters, too."

"And, we will receive better news! A verra good thought, Glynis." Heather smiled.

"If the weather held during the crossing, he could be here sooner."

"Noah has been a good son to ye, Glynis," Jamie said. "Ye are lucky to have him."

Ross nodded in agreement, remembering back to his time on the Pembroke. Noah had been a boy of twelve, light brown curls, hazel eyes full of adventure and a nose which had been a little too big for his face. Aaron swore the boy would grow into it, and indeed he had. Noah had been part of Captain Aaron Redding's life long before Glynis met him. He'd taken responsibility for the boy after his mother died. Now, he was a respected merchant captain in charge of the Pembroke, sailing the same routes Aaron did before him, keeping the Redding traditions alive.

"Dinna forget Miguel," Ross said. "Aaron Redding's gypsy uncle. He'll be here, too."

"He is more than Aaron's uncle, Ross." Glynis glared at him. "I ken ye arena fond of him but 'tis time to let go of grudges. I told yer son the same earlier this week. Och, ye MacLaren men are all the same."

"Ye canna forgive a man who believes ye are a killer, Glynis." Ross stared back at her. "He convinced Aaron I stuck a knife into the back of one of yer crew." He watched her eyes get rounder and knew he overstepped.

Noah had actually plunged the knife into Mick Cutter's back, believing the man attacked Cowan. It had become a secret between a chosen few. After the storm when they lost Aaron to the sea, the blame for the murder was placed on another crewmember who'd gone overboard. Glynis had vowed to protect Noah, swearing their inner

47

circle to tell no one. Not one man on the ship, whether he believed Mick deserved to die or not, would follow a young boy who could kill a crew member. As Noah aged, he would eventually become their captain and needed to earn their respect. According to Aaron's will, Miguel would handle the captain duties until Noah turned eighteen, then step down and return to his position as second in command.

Heather, Jamie and Brodie had no idea what happened on the ship except for the sanitized version they had been told. Ross tried to apologize with his eyes, but Glynis was not ready to accept.

Jamie cleared his throat and took a step forward. "I have something to say, and I dinna ken if ye will like it."

CHAPTER 6

*A*ll eyes went to Jamie Mercer. He usually deferred to Ross and rarely interrupted important conversations involving the family.

"Go on." Ross dipped his head once.

"If we could, Ross, you and I would be on the first ship to Scotland, but we canna go back until we are told 'tis safe. But, we can do something here. Stay together. Bond as a family." Jamie turned to Brodie. "I have a proposal, brother. It may not be the proper time to ask or speak of the forge, but I would like to rebuild it and move my family to Gregor's Cove."

A gasp came from Heather. "Oh, Jamie." She flew into his arms. "We would all be together. What a wonderful idea."

Brodie caught Ross' eye and nodded. "We will not speak of it again today, Jamie, but you have my permission to become our village's blacksmith. What of your own in Amboy?"

"My apprentice is ready to take over. He has been with me eight years since Angus left to come to Gregor's Cove. I havena discussed it with him or told him my thoughts yet. But I ken he will be happy to take on the Amboy forge as his own."

"We will help ye build a new forge, Jamie," Ross said. Inwardly, he wanted to shake the man's hand and congratulate him for thinking of the idea. "As Brodie said, we will discuss the preliminaries another day."

"We still have one more item to discuss," Heather said, looking at the group. "Nell."

"What has she done, Heather?" Glynis asked. "You keep saying she has gone mad."

"Once ye hear, sister, ye will agree."

"Are ye going to tell us or do I have to shake it out of ye?" Glynis' eyes held the spark Ross loved to see.

"Aye," Ross added. "Out with it."

"My family arrived early for the service. I told Jamie I wanted to visit Nell and see if she needed help with preparations or to watch the children. He stayed at the church with our bairns while I went to the house. When I came through the front door poor Sarah sat in a rocking chair with wee Angus in her arms wailing his head off while Nell wandered through the house, straightening and mumbling to herself."

"'Tis not enough to say she's gone mad," Glynis interrupted.

"'Tis more, sister, if ye let me tell the story."

"Get to the point, Heather. Yer as awful as Ross at storytelling. An hour goes by and he hasna found the end."

Ross pursed his lips. "I am sure I am better than what ye have described, sister."

Glynis smirked at him then smiled. "We will let Heather finish."

"All right," Heather huffed. "I will skip the part of going to the kitchen with Nell to make tea, and she made coffee instead. She served me a dry biscuit which had been sitting on the table for days, I am certain. I offered to help fix her hair, but she waved me off."

Glynis made a noise in her throat.

"I sat at her table, hoping she'd join me, and asked her plans. What would she do? I asked then assured her the village would help support her. There is always a need for maids or cooks. She stared at me as if *I* was mad. Can ye believe it? Then Nell lowered herself to a chair, leaned toward me and said, 'I am going back to Sexton Manor.'"

"No!" the group collectively said.

"Aye, she did." Heather's eyes filled with tears. "We canna let her go."

"And we canna stop her," Ross said.

"Ross, ye beef head!" Glynis yelled. "Of course, we can. I am going to speak to her now."

Juliet touched Ross' arm. "I better go with her."

---

*J*uliet was the only one who knew the truth from the day of the Sexton wedding. She saw behind Norris' protests and caught Jasper's lewd looks on the day the MacLarens took Nell from the estate ten years ago. She'd been fully aware Jasper Sexton favored Nell, especially after hearing he personally requested her to come to the main house to clean. Nell had told the story with pride, blind to the fact he would eventually have his way with her. Many English noblemen thought they had a right to pursue the help. Jasper would not be the exception.

Although Norris had been married to May, he fought too hard to keep Nell at the estate. Nell and May were just two years apart, same coloring and heart-shaped faces yet there was something about Nell which attracted a man. Juliet had seen it before. *The woman is clueless to the fact. Is she aware she is entering the lion's den?*

Juliet and Glynis walked the grounds looking for Nell and found her nowhere.

"She must be in the house," Glynis said striding to the door.

Juliet had to pick up her pace to stay with Glynis. "It may be better if I speak with her," she said to Glynis.

"What?" Glynis turned to her, fire in her eyes. "Ye dinna think I can be soft and kind?" She raised her MacLaren eyebrow. "Och, yer right. Ye speak first. Then I will have my say."

They searched the first floor, bumping into villagers who carried trays of food or helped in the kitchen. Nell was not among them. Glynis nodded toward the stairs, and Juliet followed her up to the next floor. Humming came from one room, and they peeked in the doorway. Nell sat rocking baby Angus as she stared out the window.

"Nell?" Juliet said in a quiet voice. "May we come in?"

Nell turned her head toward the sound of Juliet's voice. "Aye."

Juliet dropped down next to her, sitting on a small stool. "How are you?"

"I will be fine as soon as I send my letter to Sexton manor."

"Surely there is something we can do so you can stay instead of moving back there?"

Nell looked at her for a long moment. "There is nothing for me here."

"What will ye do at the estate?" Glynis sneered. "Ye dinna want to live there, Nell."

"I will move back to my rooms in Norris' home and assume my duties."

"Nell, are ye daft? Ye are a widow with two bairns. Jasper or Norris will certainly take advantage of you!" Glynis pushed back the black bonnet on her head and let it dangle down her back.

"Whatever do ye mean?" Nell gazed up at Glynis.

Juliet glowered at her sister-in-law. "What she means, Nell, is the state you are in, you may not realize when someone tries to take advantage of you."

Nell swung her head toward Juliet. "I do not mind extra work."

"No, lass," Glynis said and took the sleeping baby from her arms. She walked to the cradle and place little Angus in it. "Be a good laddie now." She patted his stomach and returned to where she'd stood. "Juliet and I are trying to tell ye, Nell, that those men might expect favors from ye."

"In their beds?" Nell's eyes widened. "They didna before."

"Ye lived there three months. Not long enough to be a good judge." Glynis placed her hands on her hips. "Stay here, Nell, in Gregor's Cove."

"No!" Nell jumped to her feet. "Who are ye to tell me what to do? If I want to leave this retched place ye will not stop me. I canna live here any longer."

Juliet rose from the little stool and took Nell in her arms. "You do not have to make any decisions today. Give yourself time. You have lost your husband and two daughters. Things may look different tomorrow."

"Ye also?" Nell's face twisted into a look of pain. "I ken why ye want to stay away from the estate but ye canna stop me. Norris has told me many times I could come to his home to live any time I chose. He made fun of my husband, asking if he came home covered in soot and asked how I liked washing his clothes and lying with a man who smelled of smoke. I didna like it!" Nell stamped her foot. "I was denied my love in Scotland and was contracted to marry his father instead, When I came to America, I left Sexton Estates to marry a man I didna love. Now I want to do something for me."

"Did ye forget the same man ye consider yer savior now, threw yer stillborn child into the sea?" Glynis glared at Nell.

"'Twas a bad time for us all. Norris was drunk most days on the ship. He doesna recall doing such an awful thing."

"Ye have forgiven him?" Glynis asked.

Juliet placed her hand on her sister-in-law's arm, hoping to calm her. "Glynis," she whispered.

"I...he..." Nell glowered back at Glynis. "Get out. Both of you." Her eyes came to rest on Juliet. "Get out of my house."

Juliet took Glynis by the arm before she could say another word. "Nell, we are sorry for your loss. Please remember we are here to help you." She tugged her sister-in-law to the top of the stairs where Glynis broke free.

"I willna say or do anything, Juliet. The lass has made up her mind. Let her go to the bowels of hell and live among heathens." Glynis pounded down the stairs and out the front door.

Torn, Juliet wanted to go back into the room to reason with Nell. *No, I have done all I can do.* She continued down the flight of steps, following the same path Glynis took. The long day had turned to evening, everyone was exhausted. Juliet looked to the sky and said a quick prayer, "Hopefully everything will look different with the dawn of a new day."

a few days after the funeral, the village of Gregor's Cove helped one of their own pack a wagon and leave for a new life at Sexton Estates. Jamie had negotiated a fair price for the Forbes' home and once Nell left, he made plans to move his family into the house. He told Heather he would make any changes she wanted. Thrilled to be in a larger home, Heather said she'd hold on to the promise for a later date. Jamie spent a week cleaning and painting and deemed it ready for occupancy.

The MacLarens who lived in Gregor's Cove congregated at the house to surprise the Mercers on their move-in day. Heather cried tears of joy as she hopped from the wagon.

"Sister," Glynis said and hugged her. "Ye are happy, eh?" Having made the journey from Scotland to New Jersey with Heather and Jamie, she might be the only one who knew how much this meant.

"As happy as when ye returned, Glynis, along with Ross and Juliet." Heather threw her arms around her sister.

"A toast!" Ross called. "To the MacLaren clan. We are brought together by the heart of the emerald, mighty and strong. Each stone represents a piece of the larger one that binds us together no matter where we are."

"The heart of the emerald!" Everyone chanted with smiles.

"Mum," Rory tugged on Glynis's sleeve. "Why do I not have an emerald? Ye told me Granny's story many a time yet I do not have one." He frowned. "When?"

Glynis took her son's hand and walked him to a quiet place. "Do ye remember the most important part of the story?"

Rory pressed his lips together and wrinkled his brow. "We are family?"

"Aye, 'tis important but the story starts with one large emerald with a beating heart. Each of us have a piece cut from the stone. And who do ye think is in possession of the emerald?"

"Granddad Donnach MacLaren."

"Where does he live?"

"In the Highlands of Scotland." Rory wiggled on his seat as if he had enough of her questions. "Are we going to visit him, Mum? Then I can ask for my stone."

Glynis threw her head back and laughed. "Ye never ask Donnach MacLaren for anything, lad. He would have to give ye the stone as a gift."

Rory hung his head. "Alec has one. He was going to put it in the handle of his sword that burned in the fire."

"He received the stone before his family left Scotland. Yer grandda sent one for Rosslyn and Annie but didna ken the rest of ye yet. Ye werena born."

"So, if the emerald is the heart of the family, we all need one." Rory crossed his arms with a huff. "I shall write to Granddad and tell him."

"Good luck, son," Glynis said with a smile. "Grandda would like ye, Rory. Ye have his stubbornness."

"Da says I got it from you, Mum." Rory looked up at her with his amber eyes so like his father's and showed her a toothy grin.

"Aye, I guess ye did, but I am also Donnach's daughter." Glynis gave Rory a quick squeeze. "Go play with yer cousins while I visit with yer aunts and uncles."

The end of June was almost upon them with each day becoming hotter and more humid than the last. Glynis dabbed the back of her neck with a handkerchief as she approached her brother and sisters. A cool drink was put in her hand and she said, "Thank ye, Ross." Glynis held up her glass. "A wager. Who will arrive in Perth Amboy first? My good friend Hiram Coward or my grown son who sails the seas, Noah Redding?"

"Hiram," Juliet answered. "He does not have to depend on the wind and weather."

"Ah, but it could be Noah," Heather said. "Hiram has a tendency to dawdle."

"Noah." Ross added his choice. "He docks right here in Amboy. Hiram may detour to New York to visit his brother."

"Edward kens he is welcome here also," Glynis huffed. "We have seen less of him over the years due to Penelope keeping Hiram in Boston. Hopefully it will change now."

The men bantered back and forth among themselves the reasons Noah or Hiram would arrive first. Glynis turned to her sister and Juliet. "Let us put out the food and eat. We will never get Heather moved into her house if we dinna get started."

By late afternoon the wagon was empty and taken to the barn along with two horses. The women unpacked the smaller boxes helping Heather decide where she should place things. The large furniture was left to the men while the children were in charge of clothes.

"'Tis a wonderful thing having ye close by," Heather said to Glynis and Juliet. "Ye helped settle my family into the house in less than a day. Thank ye." She put water in a kettle and hung it over the fire. "We deserve a cup of tea and I ken where to find it thanks to ye. I have never been so organized." She laughed. "It willna stay that way for long."

Juliet set the table with Heather's china teacups, sugar bowl and creamer while Glynis found biscuits left over from their dinner. Heather returned with hot water, pouring the steaming liquid over the leaves into a pear-shaped silver pot to brew.

"Ye need a proper tea table, Heather," Glynis said. "Ask Jamie to build ye one. Ye can display your finest teapot and easily find yer tea, sugar container, teaspoons and tongs."

"I can see wee James knocking it over twenty times a day in my head," Heather giggled.

"He is a year younger than Rory, Heather, and old enough to ken better." Glynis answered. "Ye treat the lad as if he was newly born."

"And ye dinna with Rory?" Heather placed a hand on her hip.

"Fine." Glynis folded her arms over her chest. "We both need to let them become men."

"It is hard to do, believe me," Juliet said. "Your boys will soon be grown like Alec and Cowan and you will wonder where the time went."

The men had gone outside to drink ale on the front porch.

Sometimes Glynis longed to join them instead of sipping tea with the womenfolk. Her mind wandered back to the days of wearing a kilt and running in the woods with Ross. They'd chase deer or rabbit, anything they could shoot at and bring home as a prize. Many of the men scoffed at the idea of Glynis joining them, but Ross always took her side. Grateful he had, she knew she could provide for the families, all of them, if ever needed. She loved her husband, but all those years ago, Glynis felt she could've lived alone in her cabin on Brodie's land and been happy.

"What are you thinking, Glynis?" Heather asked. "Usually ye say it aloud or talk to yerself." She teased.

"Och, stop it, Heather. A woman is entitled to her thoughts,"

"They must be good ones." Heather wiggled her eyebrows.

"No." Glynis shook her head. "I was thinking of another time. How much life has changed."

A sudden noise startled the women. It sounded like the men had jumped from their seats at the same time. Chairs scrapped on the wooden porch floor and the pounding of boots was heard. Shouting and whistling came through the windows, and Glynis could take no more. "Come. Let us go see what they are doing."

Glynis headed to the front door, flung it back and rushed onto the porch. In the distance she saw two people on horseback. A smile slowly spread across her face as she recognized one of the riders. "Heather! Juliet! 'Tis my lad!" She waved her hand in the air. "Noah! See, I told ye he would be first to arrive."

"Who does he have with him?" Heather asked.

"From here, it looks like a woman," Juliet answered.

"Do ye think he married?" Heather poked Glynis in the back. "Has he mentioned if he was courting someone?"

"No!" Glynis said over her shoulder. "Give him a minute before ye start asking yer questions, sister. Ye dinna have to ken his business as soon as he dismounts."

"I will give him a chance to greet everyone first, of course." Heather smirked.

Juliet appeared at Glynis' side and squeezed her arm. "Look closely at the woman, Glynis. She looks familiar. Do you think…?"

"No! I must be seeing things." Glynis' eyes filled with tears. "Mum! Ross! 'Tis Mum!"

Noah slid from the saddle and went to help the other rider to the ground. The woman wore a scarf over her head to help keep out the dust as she rode and now removed it.

"Oh Judas!" Heather yelled. "Yer right, Glynis. 'Tis Mum!"

CHAPTER 7

*H*er children swept Fiona MacLaren into a family hug all speaking at once.

"Let me catch my breath," Fiona said, kissing each of their cheeks.

"Mum is right," Ross said taking a step back. "Give her room."

"I have just made tea." Heather motioned to her front door. "Please, Mum, come in."

"I thought ya lived in Perth Amboy, Heather," Noah said, giving her a strange look. Glynis had her arm around his waist beaming with pride.

"We moved into this house today!" Heather answered with a smile then her expression changed. "Angus Forbes and two of his daughters died in a fire at the forge. 'Tis his home. Jamie will be Gregor Cove's new blacksmith."

Noah's face took on a look of disbelief. "No, it cannot be true. Angus was one of the kindest men I knew."

"'Tis true, son." Glynis grasped his arm. "Come, let us go into the house and ye can tell us why Mum is yer companion."

"I can speak for myself, daughter," Fiona said following everyone into the house.

"Indeed, Mum."

Ross hung back, pulling on Juliet's arm. "She must stay with us."

"Of course."

"Mum would never come here willingly, Juliet." Ross sucked in a breath making a noise as he let it out. "'Tis not good news she brings."

"We need to go in and discover the reason she came, Ross. You cannot stand out here and speculate."

"Yer right as always, wife." Ross took her hand. "Is she really here or 'tis a dream?"

"After all the years in the colonies it may seem like a dream, but your mother *is* here."

Once inside, Ross saw his mother had been tended to with food and drink. Glynis fawned over her surrogate son in the same way. Nerves on edge, he fought to find patience. He knew what it was like after disembarking a ship and walking into an unfamiliar land.

"Did ye stop in Amboy or come straight here?" Glynis asked Noah.

"I did as Fiona wanted," Noah answered. "She requested to be brought to Ross' home. I had no idea Heather would be here, too. Praise God, we found all of Fiona's children in one place. I had promised to run to your house, Mum," he looked at Glynis, "as soon as we got to Ross' to retrieve ya."

"And Heather?" Glynis turned toward her sister, and Ross knew she checked to see if the woman was listening.

"Her, too." Noah nodded.

The children danced around their grandmother vying for her attention. Heather's two daughters were front and center reporting news like town criers.

"I am named for Uncle Ross," Rosslyn informed her. She had the MacLaren dark hair and her father's light brown eyes. "In October I will be twelve." She lifted her chin. "Almost a woman."

"I am ten," Annie said, stepping in front of her sister. "My name is Agatha Ann after Uncle Angus' mum, but everyone calls me Annie."

Their brother James was not to be outdone. "I am named after my da."

"Ye look like yer mum," Fiona said taking James' chin in between her fingers. "Red hair and hazel eyes." She wiped a tear rolling down her cheek. "And your Grandda Donnach."

Rosslyn pulled Lizbeth into the group. "And Lizbeth, Granny, our cousin. She is nine, soon to be ten."

"What lovely hair, Lizbeth." Fiona reached out to touch her golden copper curls.

Noah, who'd been standing to the side of Fiona, stepped forward. "Lassies give the lads a turn. Your grandmama could not stop talking about Alec and Cowan. Where are they?" He craned his neck. "Ah, there." With a wave of the hand, he motioned them to come. "May I present Cowan, my lady." He bowed and extended his hand toward him.

Fiona covered her mouth as she let out a shout, "By the living God! Is that ye, Cowan?"

"Aye, madam." Cowan bent at the waist. "'Tis good to see ye again. How is my Scottish mother?"

"She is well. Gordon treats her kindly. They wed the summer ye left Glenhaven. They have two daughters and are verra happy. Gracie misses ye. After I unpack, I will give ye her letter."

"And my brother Bryce?"

"He lives in Southaven now. He went there to apprentice with yer grandda. The blacksmith shop wasna his favorite place or occupation."

"I ken." Cowan chuckled. "He wishes to be a carpenter?"

"Aye, especially when he met a lass in town."

"Did my brother marry? My mother in Scotland never mentioned he was courting someone."

Ross smiled each time Cowan referred to his Scottish mother. He considered Juliet his mother here in America, yet Gracie was his true biological one. *The lad is considerate to a fault. Careful as always not to hurt Juliet.*

"He will be married by the end of the summer, Cowan." Fiona took his hand. "'Tis so good to see ye." Her eyes lit up as Alec approached. "My daughter's son!" Tears welled in her eyes. "Ye were this high when ye left us." She held her hand low to the ground. "And now look at ye! Tall and strong. Yer beautiful hair is now brown but ye havena lost yer good looks." Fiona smiled. "We miss ye, Alec."

Alec crouched beside his grandmother and looked directly into her eyes. "I have always loved ye, Granny. It is good to see you again. But my mother stands there." He nodded toward Juliet. "You must respect that."

"Alec!" Juliet gasped.

Ross placed a hand on her arm. "The lad is right, Mum. We have lived here for ten years and many things are different. Ye remember us from the time we left Glenhaven, but as ye can see by the looks of my lads, much time has passed."

"I am sorry, Alec," Fiona stroked his head. "Forgive an old woman."

"You are not old, Granny. I will be proud to parade you through the village on my arm and introduce you as my beautiful grandmother."

Ross studied his mother. Ten years had gone by, but she barely aged a day. Her green eyes were clear and bright, her dark hair still had the few streaks of gray. "Quite bonny, Mum," he added.

Fiona made eye contact with Ross and he saw her pain and despair. He realized she had much to tell. He looked at Glynis and hoped she read his mind. Time was up. They needed details and he couldn't wait any longer. She bobbed her head once, concurring with him. "Ye are chief, Ross, here in America, we will defer to ye. My only request is ye let my lads speak with Mum first."

Glynis wrapped an arm around each of her sons and walked to her mother. "Mum, 'tis Aaron and Rory."

"I see their fathers in them," Fiona said and took the boys' hands. "I am thrilled to meet ye in person."

"You knew my father?" Aaron asked.

"I did." Fiona nodded. "I met him before Ross and his family set sail for America. We were in Crail at yer Uncle Gillander's home. Yer father was quite the gentleman and handsome, too. You have inherited one of his special qualities, his eyes. The blue is so bright and captivating. It was what I remember most about him."

"He was captain of the ship you sailed on before my brother took his place."

"Aye," Fiona answered. "'Tis a fine ship."

Aaron looked at Noah. "Where is Uncle Miguel? Why did he not come with you?"

"He is taking care of ship business. Fiona could not wait to see ya so he told us to go ahead of him."

"Ye will stay with us like always, Noah, not on the ship," Glynis said. "No arguing."

"Yes, Mum." Noah dipped his head.

"How many days before ye set sail down the coast?" Glynis asked.

"We can stay two days but will be here by August to retrieve Fiona, sail to Boston and back home to London with a stop in Crail."

"All right. We have spoken with Mum and made introductions." Glynis glanced at Ross. "We need to find seats, everyone, and let these two tell their story."

"Aye," Ross answered. "Noah? Mum? Who wishes to speak?"

"I will," Fiona said.

"Mum," Ross said. "Tell us how you came to be on Noah's ship."

"I sent a message to Gillanders asking if the Pembroke would dock in Crail this year. When the answer arrived that it would, I began to pack my things. I had to get to the ship before it set sail. Gill was to secure my passage and speak with Noah. He is a fine man, Glynis. I was a day late, yet Noah waited."

"Thank ye, Noah," Glynis said.

"I would do anything for yer family, Mum." Noah looked at the floor. "Ya know that."

"I am proud of ye, lad. Dinna be so humble."

"I have letters from Gill, Aggie..." Fiona stared at Ross. "Och, she will be devastated. The last letter from Angus said he wanted to visit."

"We will sort out the letters and what to tell Aggie once we get ye home and settled, Mum," Ross answered.

"May I continue the next part of the story?" Noah requested of Fiona.

"Please do."

Noah inhaled and let out a long breath. "The Pembroke enjoyed good weather and smooth sailing except for one mild storm and three days of no progress due to the calmness of the sea. Despite the delay we made up for it with a good western wind which arrived just in time. People who weren't sailors had begun to panic as we sat idly in the water. We let passengers off in Boston, and I encouraged those who wanted to become indentured servants and had no sponsors to stay aboard until we reach Perth Amboy." Noah searched for Brodie. "Will ya come to the Pembroke tomorrow to speak with them?"

"Of course." Brodie nodded.

"Mum," Ross said, patience fading. "What is yer reason for the visit? Ye said ye'd never cross the ocean but now yer here."

Fiona dropped her head into her hands and began to sob. Noah rushed to her side and crouched in front of her.

"My lady, do ya want me to tell them?"

"No," Fiona answered through her tears.

"Let me get ya a cup of water. More tea?"

Ross crossed the room, put his hand on Noah's shoulder and said, "I see ye care for my mother. Thank ye, but I will tend to her. Heather? More tea, please." He took his mother by the shoulders and brought her to him. "Ye dinna have to act as Donnach's wife here, Mum. Be Fiona. Ye can cry. Ye can scream. We are yer family."

Heather rushed over with her teapot to fill her mother's cup. "Here ye go, Mum. Please, dinna cry. We love ye verra much."

"She's tired, Ross," Juliet said. "She could tell us in the morning after a good night's sleep."

"No," Fiona shook her head and sank back into her chair. "I must tell ye now."

Ross pulled up a chair next to Fiona and held the teacup and saucer in front of her. "Drink, Mum. Take yer time."

Once Fiona recovered, she glanced around the room. "Most of my family is here. Seeing ye all in one place makes me realize Eva was right. Ye have yer own clan in America and have begun yer own village."

"No, Mum," Ross said. "As I said before, time and circumstance have caused this to happen. We needed to build homes, plant crops to survive. Brodie was born in America, bought this land and would have planned the village with or without us."

"'Tis peaceful here." Fiona sighed. "No English soldiers riding through the countryside as if they are looking for a Scot to do or say the wrong thing. And," she said in a low voice. "No whispers of war or an uprising."

Ross raised his eyebrows. "The Jacobites are planning another rebellion since the one in nineteen failed?"

"No," Fiona answered. "But there is always talk. Weapons stored, money raised. I fear for my only son left in Scotland. Will he go to war again? Ye ken yer father willna let him go alone. He will lead the clan."

"Mum." Ross took her hand. "Ye canna dwell on something which hasna happened or may never."

"Ye arena there, Ross. Something is going on in the bowels of the castle."

"'Tis the reason ye came. Ye fear the threat of war."

"Partly." Fiona looked at him with her green eyes filling with tears. "Wee Greer has died."

"What?" Juliet placed her hand on her chest and burst into tears. "My poor Eva."

Ross' sisters huddled together, consoling each other.

"I never got to meet the wee one," Heather wailed.

Ross had no words. A child had died. He thought his mother might say his father had taken ill, and he needed to come home. It had to be the only reason his mother sailed on a ship to America, something she sworn she'd never do. Fiona wanted him to return to Glenhaven. *How can I go?* He'd pledged his heart and soul to Glenhaven when he boarded the Pembroke ten years ago. Yet, the pull of his idyllic life in America fought with the Scottish side of him.

Juliet was by his side, crying and holding onto his arm. He wrapped her in an embrace to comfort her, wishing he could pull the whole family into his arms.

"I couldna stay," Fiona finally said after the family had calmed each other. "The castle felt like a prison, and I could barely breathe. I relived my Greer's death over and over in my mind to the point I thought I was going mad. Wee Greer's face haunts me every day. I was there as she took her final breath. Eva is a ghost of herself, walking the castle in a daze. She doesna see ye as she passes by. Her bairns beg for attention yet she doesna answer them. She lets others tend their needs. Poor Julie tries to be a mother to her younger brothers. 'Tis heartbreaking. The day wee Greer passed, Donnach locked his receiving room door and we canna get him to open even as we beg and pound all day. Cook leaves a tray on the floor outside the door hoping he will retrieve it."

Heather brought a handkerchief and placed in her mother's hand. "Mum, I am so sorry."

"I have shed enough tears, daughter. I shouldna cry. In a way, I am relieved to be here. When I saw all of ye my heart was full, so these are tears of joy and sadness." Fiona held up the embroidered cloth. "Thank ye for this." She grasped Heather's arm. "He would come out for ye, his favorite."

Startled by the statement, Ross knew he had to protect his sister. "Mum," he said in a soft voice. "Ye ken we will do everything we can to help. We will send letters and supplies back with ye. Heather and her family are safe here. 'Tis their home."

"'Tis a mother's wishful thinking, Ross, to have her family back together. Och, the damn uprising caused this! The bloody English! What more do they want? They won! They have splintered my family and threatened to hang ye as examples to everyone. The English are scared dogs."

"Now ye sound like Da." Ross lifted a corner of his mouth.

Fiona waved her hand at him. "I have lived with the old goat for too long."

"Ye will come home with us tonight, Mum, and live there for the summer. The change may do ye good."

"No!" Heather protested. "I want her to stay with us. I have the room."

Ross glared at her, and she dropped her head. "I am chief, Heather."

"I ken," Heather answered. "I would love to have her for a few days."

"And, I would love to help her settle in, Ross." Fiona patted his hand. "I dinna think I can make these old bones travel any further tonight."

"Fine. Stay here for a week then ye will move in with us."

The women of his family always found loopholes to get their way. Ross had to smile as Heather beamed, looking youthful and happy. She'd been through the most at sixteen having been ripped from her home. Many might argue he'd had the most anguish as he fought in the Uprising and lost his best friend who'd been Greer's husband. After the war he had to deal with John Alder's devious plotting to steal Juliet away from him. Some would say Glynis had seen the worst, losing Aaron twice. Yet she chose to come on this journey. Heather did not. Ross' heart always broke a little when he thought back to the day he said goodbye to Glynis, Heather and Jamie on the docks in Crail. Poor Heather looked frightened and young, too young to board the ship and travel to an unfamiliar land.

A knock on the front door interrupted the reunion. Brodie, being closest, answered and said, "Miguel! Good to see you again." He embraced the man and stepped back to let him into the room.

Miguel looked as Ross remembered him from the first time on the ship. He was a wiry, older man with long, wavy black hair who often wore a bandana wrapped around his head to keep the hair from blowing in his face. His eyes caught everyone's attention. Like his nephew, Aaron, they were a brilliant blue. He sported a beard and mustache, neatly trimmed. His skin was tanned and leathered from the sun, and he wore a small round gold earring in one ear. Fit and trim from working on the ship he looked younger than his years. From when Ross saw him last, the only change he noticed was a few more lines in Miguel's face.

Glynis rushed to him, throwing her arms around his neck. "Uncle, 'tis good to see ye. How is Noah faring as the captain of the ship?"

"You have nothing to worry about, Glynis." Miguel kissed her cheek. "Aaron would be proud."

The children gathered round Miguel as he always brought interesting treats, buying candy, food and trinkets at every port for them. They hugged and chatted until he held up his hands. "Come to Brodie's home tomorrow and I will let you see my bounty." He glanced around the room. "Where is my lady? Fiona?"

"Here, Miguel." Fiona lifted her arm from where she sat.

"Oh, my dear woman." He rushed toward her, took her hand and kissed the top. "I am sorry to have left you, but I am here now."

The room went silent. Ross felt the blood rush through his veins, his face grew hot with rage. "Step away from my mother, cad! If I'd brought my sword, the tip would be under yer nose!"

CHAPTER 8

"*R*oss! Stop yer nonsense this minute." Fiona gave him a look of disapproval. "Miguel is a friend, a verra good and kind one."

Glynis took Ross by the arm. "Ye dinna think the uncle of my dead husband would be anything but decent to our mum?" She glared at him, wanting him to see the situation as it really was. "I am sure he gave her special attention since she is my mum." She looked to Miguel.

"*Sí.*" Miguel often reverted to his native language when caught off-guard or nervous but used English better than she.

"He has done nothing wrong," Glynis said and went to Miguel's side. "The day has been long and now the night longer. 'Tis time to go home. Noah?" She looked his way. "Get yer brothers and we will walk home."

Rory hopped on Noah's back, and Aaron ran to Brodie hoping for the same ride. Glynis leaned down to kiss her mother and assure her things would be fine. "Mum, Noah can bring the family here if ye think war is looming."

"Yer da would never leave Glenhaven, Glynis. Ye ken that." Fiona patted her daughter's cheek. "Once I'm rested, we will speak more."

"Have a good night, Mum." Glynis squeezed her hand and

followed Brodie wearing Aaron on his back out the door and to the road. "Brodie!" He looked toward her. "Let Aaron walk. I need to speak with ye."

Brodie pulled his brows together and frowned when he reached her. "You look troubled, wife."

"I am." Glynis slowly shook her head. "Mum would never come to America on a whim. She plans to take Ross with her when she returns to Scotland. I feel it deep in my bones. She has the summer to convince him 'tis the right thing to do."

"Ross can make his own decisions, Glynis. We cannot interfere." Brodie stopped walking and took her by the arms. "If you are asking me what he will do, I believe he will stay. He has a plot of land which serves him well, most of his family is here, and our lives are fairly peaceful."

"Ye werena born in Scotland." Glynis made a noise in her throat. "As the eldest son, ye would have been trained from the time ye were a wee one how to be chieftain of the clan. Ross has a sense of duty and may feel he has no choice. I am afraid, Brodie." Glynis fell into his arms. "For the first time in my life I am truly frightened of what will happen in the coming months."

"We cannot predict the future, wife." Brodie kissed her forehead.

"Ye dinna understand, Brodie." Glynis looked up at her husband, heart pounding against her chest, and knew he needed a better explanation. "Yer father will probably leave ye his fortune, but 'tis not the same as what Ross must become. He will be chieftain of Clan MacLaren, laird of the land."

"Are you saying, if Donnach died, Ross would return to Scotland no matter the consequences?"

"Aye, I believe so, whether he wanted to or not."

"A heavy burden to bear." Brodie draped his arm over Glynis' shoulders and resumed his pace.

Glynis looked back down the road. "Miguel is familiar with the way to the house but I dinna see him. Do ye think he is still at Heather's?"

"I do. The man is quite smitten with your mother as I am with you."

Glynis gave Brodie an elbow to the ribs and heard a whoosh of air come from him.

"I am speaking the truth," Brodie exclaimed after catching his breath. "It does not mean the feelings are returned."

"Och, I ken."

Her family reached the blue colonial Brodie had built twelve years ago. Glynis never dreamed she'd live in the grand home except to stay as a guest. Now, she was mistress of the house.

"Lads, do not stay up long," Brodie said to his sons when they got to the porch. "You are happy to have Noah home, but you can hear his tales tomorrow."

"Just one story, Da?" Rory pleaded. "We will be very quiet."

"One story then to bed."

"Two, Da," Rory begged. "Noah will tell one, and Aaron and I will tell of the monster who lives in our woods."

"What?" Glynis looked up at Brodie.

"When the lads hear strange noises that do not belong in the forest, they blame the monster."

"I believe it is a ghost," Aaron said.

"In Scotland, 'twould be the faeries." Glynis gave him a smile.

Brodie placed his hand on Glynis' back. "Tired?"

"Not really." Glynis gave him a smile. "But I would like to go to bed." She hugged each of her sons, entered the house and went up the stairs.

Brodie stood on the braided rug in their bedroom, tugging his shirt from his pants.

"Here, let me help ye with that." Glynis slid her hands under the shirttails touching his warm skin ever so lightly. She lifted the material up and over Brodie's head in one swift movement.

"You never cease to amaze me." Brodie dropped his head and found her lips.

Glynis' body responded to the kiss as all thoughts from the evening escaped her mind. "Let me finish undressing ye." She slid her hands around the top of his breeches and Brodie gasped as he inhaled.

"Ye like that," she whispered, wiggling out of her dress and shift.

She crushed her body against his bare chest and looked into his eyes. "I love ye, Broden Gregor."

"And I, you, Glynis Gregor." His hungry lips found hers as he backed toward the bed, pulling her on top of him as he tumbled onto the mattress.

Glynis giggled and rolled to her side. "I want to think of nothing but us, Brodie. Let us enjoy the night." She kissed his lips, so he could not ask why. What she wanted to tell him could wait another day.

*R*oss paced through the house unable to sleep. Fiona's arrival had unsettled him, and he was quite aware of what she wanted. He needed to come to terms with the truth. Life in Gregor's Cove was over the moment his mother stepped through Heather's doorway. He'd felt it the minute he saw her. She wanted him to come home to Scotland. Ross had pledged his life to his clan and Glenhaven, missing the Highlands every time he stepped foot in the woods. "Why do I feel so angry?"

Warm arms slipped around his waist, and he caught Juliet's vanilla scent. "Angry? What troubles you?"

"You should be asleep, wife."

"How can I sleep when my husband walks the house?" Juliet tapped his arm, so he would face her. "Tell me what is wrong."

"Think, Juliet. Mum did not come all the way from Scotland to visit family. She'd never cross the ocean, especially by herself. Ye heard her say she was too old for such travel and wouldna leave Da alone in Glenhaven before we left." Ross drew in a breath and exhaled. "I never thought I would go home, Juliet. We have made a good life in Perth Amboy, and Eva was right, most of our family is here. I can only say it to ye, my love. I dinna want to go back but I ken I must."

"Oh, Ross." Juliet dove into his arms. "Wherever you go, I will follow. If you must, we will return together."

Ross took her by the arms, pulling Juliet back to look into her eyes. "Ye are happy here?"

"Yes." Juliet glanced away.

"How can I take ye from yer happiness? The last ten years have been some of the best."

"We will keep them as good memories, Ross." Juliet took his face in her hands. "Besides, we do not know why your mother has come. She did not say a word about you returning to Scotland. Let her enjoy the summer in Gregor's Cove, regain her strength from the crossing and be part of our daily life."

"'Tis a good idea. I am making assumptions. Perhaps she came for advice or needed to get away after wee Greer's death." *I will let Juliet think I am pacified. No need for her to worry…yet.*

"Fiona was close to Greer and now lost a granddaughter with the same name. I am sure it stirs old feelings."

"Aye." Ross nodded and kissed Juliet's forehead. "Have the lads and Lizbeth settled in for the night?"

"Hours ago. It is almost daybreak." Juliet kissed his lips, making Ross hunger for more.

"May I take ye to bed?"

"Yes," Juliet whispered.

In one fluid movement, Ross lifted Juliet from the floor, cradling her in his arms. For one sweet hour, he hoped to clear his mind of the dramatic evening and make love to his wife. His sweet, beautiful, strong Juliet.

Once he arrived at the bedroom door, he let Juliet slide to the floor. Ross closed the door behind them and followed her to their bed. He burned with desire, a feeling which never waned after all their years of marriage.

Juliet's chestnut hair floated down over her shoulders as she undid her braid. Her shift dropped to the floor, and she stood in front of him offering her body and soul. He could never love another woman the way he loved her. "I love ye, Juliet, now and forever."

"And I, you." Juliet held out her arms as she slipped onto the bed. "Come to me and forget about your problems for a time. Can you do that?"

"Aye." Ross nodded and slid into her arms, silently thanking King George for sending her to him.

"*Mum!* Mum! Are you in the kitchen?" Rory yelled, pounding down the steps.

"Aye, lad, and stop yer screaming. Ye'll wake the dead."

"No, I will not." Rory stood in the entryway and folded his arms across his chest. "They are already dead."

"Did ye wash?" Glynis pointed the wooden spoon she held at the boy.

"Oh, yes, I did."

"Then why do I see Aunt Heather's jam on yer cheek from last night?" Glynis closed one eye and gestured to the bucket. "Wash yer face and do a good job. Dinna just touch yer cheeks with water."

"Aww, Mum, you spoiled the fun."

"How could I? 'Tis only you and me in the kitchen."

"Aaron and I want to take Noah in the woods and hunt for the monster. The jelly on my cheek might be bait. So, do I have to wash?"

Glynis held back a chuckle and pointed to the bucket.

"Noah said he'd take a rifle and shoot it." Rory danced around the pail of water as he chatted. "Aaron said it is a ghost and a bullet will not kill him." He glanced up at Glynis. "What do you think, Mum?"

"I think 'tis a mountain man who lives deep in the woods and prefers not to be bothered by curious lads."

"If he lives deep in the woods, Mum, why is he coming so close to Gregor's Cove?"

"Och, I dinna ken. Rory, ye ask too many questions."

Brodie strode into the room and drew Glynis into a hug, kissing her on the neck.

"Ooh!" Rory wiggled his fingers and widened his eyes. "You're in love."

"Aye, lad, we are." Brodie took a towel and wiped his son's face. "Is that what you do in the schoolyard? Tease the other lads and lassies?"

Rory giggled. "Maybe."

"Then the monster will have to get you." Brodie made a claw-hand and went for his son's belly making him laugh until he fell on the floor.

74

"Enough, Broden!" Glynis blew a wisp of hair from her eyes. "Ye are worse than the lads."

"Mum," Rory said, picking himself up off the floor. "Can we take some food with us? We could be gone for the day."

Glynis looked at Brodie and shrugged. "If Noah goes with ye, then aye. But I want ye home for supper." She glanced toward the kitchen entryway when she heard Aaron and Noah's voices. "Ye are going monster hunting?"

"Ya." Noah smiled. "I will help my little brothers vanquish the forest monster as I have done to the one at sea."

"Och, did ye now?" Glynis shook her head. "When did it happen? I dinna remember fighting any."

"A few years back, Mum when ya were safely on land." Noah winked.

"Sit down, lads, and have yer porridge." Glynis placed her hand on Noah's shoulder. "Thank ye for doing this."

Noah was a grown man of twenty-three, two years older than Cowan. He did not have to play with the boys, and Glynis appreciated the gesture. She would have loved more of his time, but his brothers adored him and never got to spend much time in his presence.

"I was hoping ye would have a story for yer mum," Glynis said. "One which ended with marriage and bairns."

"Mum!" Noah rolled his eyes. "How can I court someone and be captain of a ship?"

"Yer father managed."

"He was lucky." Noah nudged her when she took a seat next to him at the table. "He found the most special woman in the world. I cannot seem to find anyone who wants to sail the seas."

"The wife doesna have to go to sea, Noah. She could live in the London townhouse."

"I would see her four or five months of the year?" Noah lifted a shoulder. "I would prefer her to sail with me."

"Then I will pray you find the right woman."

"Are you finished?" Rory said with an exasperated tone. "You are taking too long, Noah."

"I am ready, little brother. Lead the way." Noah slid from the bench and kissed Glynis on the cheek. "Thank you, Mum. I do not think I will fire a rifle today, but I will enjoy the hunt."

"Remember to be here by supper. I expect yer Uncle Hiram today. He plans to leave the heat of the city and stay with us for the next two months."

"Aaron told me he will return to Boston with him."

"Aye, to further his studies, as he did for his cousins, Cowan and Alec."

"And me!" Rory jumped around them, porridge stuck to the corner of his mouth.

"Not yet but one day." Glynis licked her finger and rubbed the boy's mouth.

"Yuk!" Rory pushed at her hand.

"Stand still or it will take longer."

"Please, Noah, can we leave before Mum dunks me in a tub of water?" Rory pulled away from Glynis, making her laugh.

"Tis a good idea, son." Glynis looked around the kitchen. "What did I do with the tub?" She heard feet pound on the wooden floor and when she looked back to where Rory stood, he was gone. "I hope they took food," she said to Brodie.

"Aaron and I readied a pail while you cleaned our other son."

"Oh, Brodie, I think the good Lord sent him to remind us to have patience."

"I believe He did, Glynis." Brodie chuckled. "I am going out to the barn and into the fields. If Hiram arrives, come for me."

"I will." Glynis kissed his cheek and saw him to the door. "Now I have to clean the kitchen since no one else is here to do it."

Once she finished, Glynis made a cup of tea to take to the front porch. She'd darn socks and sew patches on pant legs while she watched for Hiram. "I'll keep the kettle hot. Hiram likes his tea." She smiled at the thought of her friend, an Englishman who her father would call a bloody Sassenach.

Glynis had learned the world held more people than Scots, a lesson Donnach MacLaren would shun. She smiled as she thought of her father questioning her choices of companionship when she and Aaron had dined with the family at Uncle Gill's home in Crail. Yet, he had every right to his suspicions. Donnach had his clan to protect, and the English were always a constant threat. Since the Uprising of Fifteen and the Nineteen, another rebellion which had been quickly squashed, they'd become more vigilant. She and Ross had spoken of another war in the future, and he told her something which made tingles go up her spine.

"Between us, Glynis," Ross had said. "Da is stockpiling weapons in the bowels of the castle. I am sure there is also a chest filled with coin to use when the time comes."

Glynis' heart had stopped at that moment. She thought of her sons, her nephews and the Scots in the village. If they were back home, they would be recruited by the Jacobites to fight. "Werena these wars enough?"

CHAPTER 9

"Good day to you, Glynis." Hiram's voice interrupted her thoughts. "I hope you were not asleep. You did not look when I rode up to the house, so I treaded carefully."

"Oh!" She put her hand to her heart. "Hiram! You startled me."

"My apologies." Hiram bent at the waist.

"No." Glynis waved her hand. "Dinna be sorry." She jumped from her chair and down the steps, throwing her arms around his neck. "'Tis good to see ye, my friend. Come, sit. Ye are here sooner than I expected."

"Thank you." Hiram settled into a chair on the porch. "I did not want to wait for my trunk to be loaded on a wagon from the ferry. Imagine my surprise when I went to the forge and found Jamie's apprentice and not Jamie. The man lent me a horse, but I insisted on payment."

"We will return it for ye. And yer trunk?"

"On its way. I again paid handsomely to have it delivered here."

"Och, where are my manners. Let me get ye a cup of tea and some biscuits." Glynis went into the house, glad she'd prepared food in advance. She placed everything on a tray and returned to the porch. "How are ye faring, Hiram? Since…"

"Penelope's death?" Hiram closed his eyes and leaned against the back of the chair. "I am at peace."

"Do you think ye will ever marry again?" Glynis asked.

Hiram sat up, wide-eyed, pushing his round-framed glasses up his beak nose. "I have not given it much thought. Penelope was quite demanding...and kept me from my friends."

"So ye will finally admit it."

"Yes." Hiram dropped his head. "I believe she was jealous of you."

"Me? No." Glynis shook her head. "Penelope and her refined ways are much preferred by most."

"Then I am in the minority." Hiram looked at Glynis from the corner of his eye which made her laugh. "Now, tell me why Jamie Mercer is no longer Perth Amboy's smithy?"

Glynis gave him a short account of the last few weeks, the fire, Angus' death, Nell's departure and her mother's arrival. "I ken ye would be here so I didna write."

"Poor Angus. He was a kind soul." Hiram looked at her intently with his dark, beady eyes she once thought were cold and calculating as Jasper Sexton's. Instead she discovered they were filled with kindness and love. "And your mother came from Scotland! What wonderful news. When do I meet her?"

"She is staying with Heather at the moment." Glynis searched for the right words. "She may not take kindly to ye, Hiram. Ye are a Sassenach and sworn enemy of my people."

"One tends to forget those things in the colonies. I will try my best to show her how a true Englishman behaves."

"Try as ye may, be prepared." Glynis lifted one brow.

"Oh!" Hiram held up his pointer finger. "I brought something." He dug in the bag he'd brought with him. "My order arrived with the Pembroke when it docked in Boston earlier this month. I cannot wait for you to see." He held the item up, smiling.

"A book?" Glynis squinted to read the title.

"Yes, I ordered two. One for myself, and one for the boys. *Gulliver's Travels* or *Travels into Several Remote Nations of the World. In Four Parts. By Lemuel Gulliver, First a Surgeon, and then a Captain of Several Ships* by

Jonathan Swift. It is quite popular since its publication. Everyone wants a copy of the satirical prose. I've read it twice."

"Thank ye for thinking of the lads. Give it to Aaron first, he will read it in less than a week. Rory?" Glynis raised one shoulder. "Who kens?"

"Ah, Aaron." Hiram tapped his fingertips together. "He will make quite the scholar. I cannot wait to take him to Boston to live. The house will not seem as empty. Cowan and Alec have been wonderful guests, but Penelope was there too. Now it seems too quiet. I rattle around the rooms with nothing to do and there is no one available for conversation."

"Ye have yer servants, Hiram. Ye are not alone."

"You know what I mean."

"I do, but ye ken how I feel about servants and slaves. They are people, too, and deserve to be treated as such." Glynis let out a breath, aware he had heard but wouldn't comment. "Besides, Cowan may return to Boston with Alec. I heard he wants to finish his studies and become a lawyer."

"We spoke of it. I am glad he made the right decision to pursue his education. I will do everything I can to help him. Has he chosen to live in Boston?"

"Juliet and Ross will not like it, but yes, he feels 'tis the place to start a law practice."

"He will always have Gregor's Cove, Glynis, and will return often."

"When all three return in September, ye will have a houseful of noisy lads."

Hiram pressed his lips together. "At times, Penelope wished for peace and quiet, but I enjoyed them."

A mixture of children's voices with a man's deeper tone stopped their conversation. Rory was the first to round the corner of the house and yelled to Glynis, "We almost caught him, Mum!"

"Rory, where are yer manners?"

"Oh! I did not see you, Uncle Hiram. Good day!" Rory hopped up the steps and plopped into Hiram's lap. "We almost caught a monster!"

"I see you have not changed, Rory." Hiram hugged the boy to him. "I have brought you and your brother something."

"What?" Rory's eyes shone with excitement and Hiram placed the book on the boy's lap. "A book?" He wrinkled his nose and made a face.

"Not just any book, my boy. *Gulliver's Travels.* Do you know Gulliver washes up onshore after a shipwreck in a land called Lilliput where people are this big?" Hiram held up his thumb and forefinger with a space of six inches between them.

"Really?"

"Yes, and there is more, but you will have to read to find out."

"Being the eldest, I feel I should read it first," Aaron said with a laugh. "Good day to you, Uncle Hiram. It is good to see you." He bent at the waist.

"No hugs for your uncle anymore?" Hiram asked then said with a nod, "You are becoming a man. You will do well in Boston."

"Thank you, sir. I intend to make you proud."

Rory wiggled around to face Hiram. "We almost caught the monster."

"I see we have returned to the subject at hand." Hiram raised his eyebrows as he glanced at Glynis and chuckled. "You have a monster in your woods?"

"The lads insist we do. I say 'tis a mountain man."

"We found no one, Mum," Noah said, nodding at Hiram. "Good day to ye, Hiram. I have read *Gulliver's Travels,* too. He is a man after my own heart."

"Indeed," Hiram said. "He liked adventure and to sail the seas. I hope you never encounter the likes of the Yahoos." He chuckled.

"Perhaps I shall." Noah laughed. "You never know."

---

*L*onger days and warmer temperatures became the norm as the week went by. Ross and Juliet readied the special guest room for Fiona, utilizing the time to make it comfortable. He'd let his mother stay with Heather as promised and now it was time to bring her home. Due to their location, Fiona could easily walk to

Heather's or Glynis' house to visit so he felt he wasn't taking his mother away from his sister.

"A verra fine job, if I say so myself," Ross said, admiring their work.

"I am glad you thought of an extra room for guests when you built the house, Ross, but we have left it empty for so many years, never expecting any. Luckily, I worked on a quilt when I found the time and Keith had a bedframe available at his shop."

"Gregor's Cove is becoming a thriving village, Juliet. We dinna have to do all the work ourselves." Ross placed his hands on his hips. "Mum will like the first floor off the kitchen. The bairns willna be in her way, and she'll have some privacy."

"I do not think she minds the children. Lizbeth has gone to visit her each day. I am glad she is getting to know her granny." Juliet smoothed a crocheted lace runner on the dresser. "We can put her bowl, pitcher and towels here."

"We have everything in place. Ye did a fine job on the quilt, Juliet. Are ye ready to get Mum?" Ross asked. "I may need help prying her from my sister's death grip."

"Ross!" Juliet giggled. "And, yes, I am ready to bring Fiona home."

Ross had the horse and wagon in front of the house waiting to take them down the road. When they reached Heather's, he was surprised to see other family members' horses tied to their hitching post.

"Ross is finally here, Mum!" Heather came out to the porch. "Come, we have been waiting."

Ross looked at Juliet, wrinkling his brow.

"I heard nothing," she said with a lift of a shoulder.

Glynis, Brodie and their boys greeted them when they entered the house.

"No Hiram?" Ross said to his sister.

"We told him we had an important meeting at Heather's and would return soon. He said he'd rest while we are gone. The lads have exhausted him this week, insisting he hunts for the monster in the woods each day. He may wish to return to Boston soon."

"Lord Hiram Coward runs through the forest with the lads?" Ross chuckled.

"He doesna mind although he grumbles. Secretly I think he enjoys it."

"Ross," Fiona said with a wave. "Sit by me."

Taken by surprise, Ross did as he was told. "Mum, is something wrong?" he whispered.

"No, 'tis quite the opposite," she said with a smile and glanced around the room. "I think we're all here."

"Cowan is not, Granny," Lizbeth said.

Ross looked his daughter's way and saw Alec standing with her. "All right. What is going on?"

"With Lizbeth's help, we are going to have a ceremony today. She made sure the family would be here when you came to retrieve me," Fiona answered then smiled as she gazed out over her family. "I need Lizbeth, Rory, Aaron and James to step forward." She looked at them with love. "Listen carefully, my sweets. I told my bairns this story when they were wee ones. 'Tis called *The Heart of the Emerald*. I placed five emerald necklaces and five pins on a table in front of them. The two extra necklaces were for my sons' future wives. The pins had the MacLaren crest embedded in them. They would be used to seal letters, stamp documents, and adorn our plaid. Each one had an emerald placed in the crest. But!" She held up a finger. "There was something special about each gemstone. Do ye ken what 'tis?"

Lizbeth jumped up and down. "I do, Granny, but you have to tell the story."

"Aye, Lizbeth, I do." She winked. "One emerald had been divided into smaller stones. The original stone had one soul, one heart. When it was cut, its heart and soul was shared amongst the smaller gems. When they are brought together, it makes us one." Fiona opened her hand which held four emeralds. "Look closely. Do ye see it?"

Rory wrinkled his nose and sniffed. "I do not see anything, Granny."

"Then ye need to look closer." Fiona paused. "Each stone has a heartbeat, Rory. 'Tis yer turn to receive a piece of our MacLaren gem." She gestured to Aaron and placed one in his hand. "Rory. James." Fiona called for them to come to her.

After giving the two boys their gems, Fiona took Lizbeth's hand.

She put the emerald in the palm of the girl's hand and wrapped her fingers around it. "Yer grandda sent these with his love."

A gasp and sob came from Heather. "Oh, Mum, thank ye. Rosslyn and Annie received theirs from Ross when he arrived, but James never had one."

"My bairns are honored," Glynis said, walking up behind her sons and placing her hands on their shoulders.

"I should like a necklace like my mum's," Lizbeth replied with a grin which made everyone laugh.

"I will start work on it immediately, niece," Jamie called to her.

"A wonderful surprise, Mum." Ross kissed her cheek. "We are united as one once again."

"It took some convincing, but yer Da kent it was best if I brought them with me." Fiona took his hand. "My work here is done. I have given out the letters I brought, except for yers." She placed the folded paper in the hand she did not hold. "From yer Da." Fiona leaned across her son to speak to Juliet. "I am sorry, I tried to get Eva to write to you. She is still in such a state. We worry she will never be the same again."

"It is all right, Mum. I have started to write letters for everyone in the family, including Eva, and will have them ready before you leave."

Fiona stayed silent and sat back in her chair. "I am glad to be here with all of ye. Please visit me at Ross' home."

"Ye can come to my house whenever ye wish, Mum," Heather said. A tear escaped her eye as she rushed to mother, crouching in front of her.

"Now daughter, I am only going a half mile or so." Fiona brushed Heather's red hair back from her eyes.

"I ken, but I loved having ye here."

"Heather," Glynis said. "Mum hasna visited my house yet and ye dinna see me crying."

"Och, Glynis, ye and Mum…"

"Have mended ways," Fiona said, taking Heather's chin and lifting so their eyes met. "Yer sister loves me verra much and I love her. She has different ways about her, 'tis all."

"I ken and I am sorry, Glynis." Heather looked up at her with her hazel eyes filled with tears. "Forgive me?"

"There is nothing to forgive. I never told ye what happened in Crail. Mum and I came to an understanding."

"Oh, Mum, ye must visit Glynis' home as soon as ye can," Heather exclaimed. "'Tis a lovely home which Brodie painted blue."

"From what I hear she has a Sassenach living under her roof," Fiona said with a chuckle.

"We have given him a week to adjust, Mum. He is fearful to meet ye after we told him stories of what ye and Da would like to do to the English," Glynis replied.

"Och." Fiona waved her hand. "If he is Edward Coward's brother, how bad can he be?"

Everyone laughed, giving Ross a chance to interrupt. "I'll give ye time to say yer goodbyes, Mum. Jamie and I will load yer trunk onto the wagon." He had a sudden urge to leave, find a quiet place in the barn and read his letter.

Ross sat impatiently waiting for his family to come from the house and get in the wagon. He grumbled as they took their time climbing in and finding a seat. Glynis, Brodie and the boys rode their horses alongside until they reached his home and rode on to their farm. Aaron and Rory kept turning and waving making the process of disembarking longer. Ross hopped down and went around to the other side of the wagon to help his mother once the Gregors were finally too far to continue the game.

"Mummy?" Lizbeth tugged on Juliet's sleeve as they walked to the house. "Cowan never came to Auntie Heather's."

"He is courting Gwen, my darling."

"But he missed the ceremony and did not get an emerald. Does he have one?"

Juliet looked to Ross for an answer, eyes widening in fear of his answer.

"Aye, Cowan has had an emerald for a verra long time, Lizbeth. Yer grandda gave him a pin the day after he rescued me from prison."

"I never knew. The man has a soul after all," Juliet whispered to Ross.

"Donnach can be soft hearted when needed," Ross said under his breath. "Now, if ye will excuse me, I will take Mum's trunk to her room and go to the barn."

"To read?" Juliet smiled.

"Ye ken me well, wife." Ross hopped from the wagon, lifted the trunk on his shoulder and walked around to the back of the house. Going in the kitchen door, he went down a hall to the guest bedroom. He set the trunk on the floor and felt in his pocket to see if the letter was still there. "I ken what ye will say, Da, before I even read this."

Ross left the house and found a quiet spot in the barn. He sat on a bale of hay, broke the seal and read:

To my eldest son, Ross.

If yer reading this, yer mother has made it safely to America. Only ye ken if she did, I will wonder until the day she returns or I receive a letter from ye. I fought her decision to visit the colonies, but in the end, Fiona kens what is best. She is a stubborn woman and insists she will bring ye back to Scotland, Ross, if ye still consider Glenhaven home. Many years have passed, and we are strangers. I dinna ken what is in yer heart.

When Eva was in her right mind, she always said ye had a clan of yer own in America. From what we have read in yer letters, I must agree. I canna believe how many Scots live in Perth Amboy or Gregor's Cove and are ones we ken! But, no matter how many Scots live in this new land, I could never leave Glenhaven. Ye ken it, son. Whatever happens here, I will stay and see it through. I want ye to make the best decision for the family when the time comes. Glenhaven is yers, and there must be a part of ye that longs to see her again.

Your father,
Donnach

"Och, Da!" Ross threw the paper to the ground. "I already feel guilty. Ye have made it worse." He rubbed his face with a hand, picked up the letter and returned it to a pocket. "I will make the best decision, the right one when the time comes. I am torn between two countries, loyal to both. Could this be any harder?"

"Da?"

Ross looked up to see Lizbeth standing in the doorway. "Aye, lass?"

She ran to him and wrapped her arms around his neck, slipping onto his lap. "I am sorry. I did not mean to eavesdrop. I only heard you feel guilty. Did Granddad's letter make you sad?"

"'Tis hard, Lizbeth, having family in two places."

"Granddad should move here. Granny loves Gregor's Cove."

"Two things ye will learn about yer grandda, if ye should ever meet him. First, he is a stubborn man and would never change his ways. The other? He is chieftain of Clan MacLaren, responsible for the people of our village and caretaker of the land."

"Is he like a king?"

"Aye, of his land. So ye see, he wouldna leave."

"He is probably sad, too, Da. We live far away, and he has not met most of his grandchildren. If he is king, he cannot leave Glenhaven like Granny did."

"Yer right, Lizbeth. Thank ye for helping me see his perspective. Grandda has many obligations, ones which can wear on him. He always had his family around him until we were forced to leave. I am sure he feels he walks the earth alone."

"He has Uncle Duncan."

"He does, but I am the eldest."

"One day you will be king?"

"Maybe, my sweet lass. 'Tis a fate I was destined for but now dinna wish to come true."

CHAPTER 10

The next morning Glynis arrived at her brother's door to escort Fiona to the Gregor home, staring at the weathered paint on its frame longer than she should. Her stomach clenched into a tight ball as she realized she'd never been alone with her mother or had a one-on-one conversation as an adult.

"Och, Glynis, ye have looked a wild boar in the eye, this canna be much different," she scolded herself. Her hand floated over the doorknob, she willed it to grasp on, and turned the handle. "Hey ho?"

"In the kitchen," a voice answered.

Glynis followed the sound to find Juliet and Fiona having tea.

"Would you like to join us?" Juliet smiled, aware of Glynis' dilemma and fear of being alone with her mother. They'd spoken of her relationship with Fiona on the Pembroke, and many times since then.

"Thank ye, no. I will wait for Mum to finish and be on our way."

"I am ready now, daughter. Juliet, thank ye for the tea. 'Tis wonderful to sit and enjoy a cup."

"You are welcome, Mother." Juliet looked to Glynis. "Should I set a place for Mum for supper?"

"No, she will eat with us and one of the boys will escort her home."

Glynis stared at Juliet, trying to remember topics she had suggested for the walk back to her house.

"Fiona, you must tell Glynis about the renovations you have done to the castle. I have told her about the ones completed while Ross and I still lived there but your letters never mentioned you continued the project."

"Doesna the Bible say not to boast?" Fiona smiled.

"Mum," Glynis answered. "Ye are not boasting if ye tell yer daughter of yer good fortune. I would love to hear."

"Let us get started then." Fiona rose from her chair, straightened her MacLaren green and blue plaid sash over the green linen day dress she wore and slipped her arm through Glynis's. "Juliet has told ye of the new foyer, drawing and dining rooms and how James Gibbs, our architect, had the main staircase torn down and rebuilt it. We had to use the servants' steps during the project."

"Aye, Juliet told me some, but I would like to hear you describe it."

The sun had warmed the day and humidity had already set it. Glynis set the pace with her mother, not wanting to hurry her. The weather, compared to Scotland, was different in New Jersey. Most summer days ranged from mild to warm in the Highlands. The brown and gray of winter would disappear, and the hills were replaced with green and wildflowers as far as the eye could see. In Gregor's Cove, the family experienced sweltering temperatures during the months of July and August, never quite getting used to it. June was not much better. They enjoyed the spring days more so than the summer but found solace during the hottest days under the bountiful trees which graced the land.

"As I was telling Juliet, Eva and I worked on the second-floor apartments. All our gray stone walls have been covered with cream paneling and each set of rooms received their own color palette." Fiona shook her head. "I dinna ken why we worked so hard to decorate empty rooms. My hopes were one day they would be filled again."

"They could be, Mum. Julie is twelve and within a few years might marry. The lads will follow."

"Ye ken what I mean, Glynis."

"I do, and I am sorry we canna fulfill yer dream." The house came into view and before they reached it, Glynis wanted to speak with her mother in private. "Mum, tell me the truth. What is happening at Glenhaven? Is Da ill or stubborn? And is it true he is stockpiling weapons?"

"Oh, my, so many questions." Fiona brought her hand to her cheek. "Donnach isna ill but always stubborn. He needs to eat more instead of drink. The man is thinner than you remember. When he rises in the morning, he heads straight to his reception room and stays there well into the night. Cook places meals outside his door yet never sees him take them. But the tray disappears. Sometimes, late at night when I canna sleep, I walk the halls and stand in one of the turrets, staring at the dark sky. When the moon is bright, I sometimes see Donnach outside, darting about as if he is stalking prey."

"He will not listen to ye, Mum? Ye could always make him see reason."

"No." Fiona hung her head. "The only one who can get a response is Julie. He will let her into his room for minutes at a time and when she comes out, we pounce on the poor thing to ask questions. She says they mostly play games, or he tells her a story. Julie says he hugs her tight and sometimes calls her our firstborn daughter's name...Greer."

"Oh!" Glynis felt a tug on her heart.

"There is not much more to tell, I am sorry. Your brother Duncan tries his best to tend to the daily duties of the castle and village. He is verra good with the people and assures them Donnach is fine."

"And the weapons?"

Fiona pulled Glynis closer. "Dinna tell anyone, Glynis, of what I am about to say. I have seen the weapons with my own eyes. Remember the hidden room in the cellar? We had to put Ross there when John Alder looked for him. I thought it was empty but noticed the barrels in front of the door appeared to be stacked differently from time to time. One night when the castle was quiet, I waited in a turret which faced the road to the village and caught sight of a wagon rumbling toward the castle. Donnach greeted the men, and I watched them carry sacks inside. I snuck downstairs and followed them to the cellar. The barrels to the room had been set aside and the door wide open. 'Tis when I saw the weapons, but no one saw me."

Glynis was proud of her mother. If she did not get the answers she wanted, she'd find another way. "I am more like ye than ye think." She chuckled.

"Perhaps."

"We have never spoken as two women, Mum. I am glad we had the chance." Glynis noticed the knot in her stomach had disappeared during their talk.

"I am, too, my dear daughter. I am most proud of ye. What I mistook for defiance served ye well. Ye lost yer first husband twice. Most women would have never recovered. Yer determination in all things got ye through a terrible time. Look at ye. Mum of two strapping lads, both handsome in their own right." Fiona held up her pointer finger. "There is something about the eldest, Glynis. Those eyes. I have never seen such bonny blue ones until I met his da. The lasses will all want to be courted by Aaron Gregor, mark my words."

"Och, Mum, 'tis the granny in ye. Ye think all the bairns are the best."

"No, Glynis. Remember I havena seen them or watched them grow. I met them as they are today. Each is already a person." Fiona poked her. "Ye have yer hands full with the wee one, Rory, eh?"

They laughed as they walked toward the house, Glynis now eager to show her mother the house she called a home.

---

*B*rodie finished his morning chores and checked on the boys to see if they had completed the tasks he'd given them. "Well done, lads. I think your mum has had enough time with Granny. Do you think we should join them?"

"Aye, Da." Rory wiped his dirty hands on his shirt, making Brodie cringe. "I am ready."

"After you change into clean clothes, you will be." Brodie inspected Aaron from top to bottom. "You look clean, lad, did you do any work?" He teased.

"You know I did." Aaron laughed. "I worked harder than my little brother."

"You did not." Rory slapped his hands on his hips.

"But you win, Rory." Aaron gave him a push. "In the dirty pig category." He ran as Rory chased him.

"Lads! Enough. We will go in the back door and Rory will take off his shirt. Hopefully yer mum and Granny are on the front porch."

As luck would have it, Glynis was giving Fiona a tour of the house when they arrived. Brodie greeted his mother-in-law with a quick "good day" and hurried into the boys' bedroom to retrieve a shirt for his youngest son.

"Rory?" Glynis caught his eye as Brodie slipped past them to go downstairs.

"Aye. He will be presentable when you come down."

"We are coming now," Glynis answered.

Brodie gestured to Rory and threw the shirt in his direction. "Put this on."

"Granny!" Aaron called and ran to her.

Not to be outdone, Rory with one arm in a sleeve and material from the body of the shirt across his face, tried to follow. He bumped into a table, knocking a vase from the top. Brodie lunged forward to catch it in time.

"My, you do have to watch him," Fiona said. "You remind me of your cousin, Edward."

"I would like to meet him," Rory answered, wrapping his arms, now both in sleeves, around his grandmother's legs.

"He lives in Scotland, lad, but I ken he would love to meet ye, too." Fiona looked at Brodie and Glynis. "I would love to spend time with the lads. Why dinna ye go for a walk or ride?"

"Thank you, Fiona. It is quite the kind gesture," Brodie said. "But you have just arrived. We could never take advantage of the kind offer."

"Ye need time together. 'Tis good for a marriage. I ken. I had five bairns!" Fiona smiled. "I did the same for Heather and Jamie. Each day I would tell them to go off on their own and I stayed with the bairns." She gave Brodie a sincere look. "I wouldna have said it if I didna mean it."

"Tis a wonderful offer, Mum," Glynis said. "I agree with Brodie. We wouldna want to leave ye so soon."

"I will sit on yer porch, enjoy the morning sun and watch the lads play."

"I can tell Granny about *Gulliver's Travels*, Mum." Aaron's eyes shone with delight. "I have read it once and will read it again after Rory finishes."

"I havena heard of the book," Fiona said.

"Uncle Hiram brought it for us," Rory said and stuck out his chest. "He thinks I am old enough to read it."

Fiona looked at Glynis. "I almost forgot Hiram Coward was here. I would like to meet the man."

"He went to the village, Mum and will be home in time for dinner."

"What is for dinner?" Fiona raised one eyebrow and looked at Brodie. "Should I check in on it or is my daughter a fine cook?"

Brodie held back his laughter and waited for his wife to answer.

"Ye can check the pot, Mum, and give it a stir if you wish." Glynis walked over to Brodie and took his hand. "We will go for an hour but 'tis all."

"We will be fine, dinna worry." Fiona waved a hand as the couple headed for the kitchen.

Glynis grabbed a blanket, and Brodie took a jug of ale. "We may get thirsty," he said.

"Let us walk to the stream, Brodie, sit and enjoy the coolness of the woods."

---

*I*t was the perfect time to speak with Brodie. Ever since her mother arrived, no matter how much her brother fought the idea, Glynis quickly realized he would return with Fiona to Scotland. For the past week, Glynis had various conversations in her head of how and when she would speak to Brodie on the subject. Her mother handed her the opportunity.

After spreading the blanket and settling in, Glynis scooted closer to Brodie. "I have been wanting to speak with ye in private. 'Tis hard to do with two lads underfoot."

Brodie chuckled. "I have to agree." He pulled back to look at her. "You sound serious. What is wrong?"

"Nothing is wrong. I dinna ken how to say this." Glynis bit into her top lip and closed her eyes. "If Ross returns to Scotland with Mum, I must go with him."

"What?"

His reaction startled Glynis, and she opened her eyes. The look of anger on Brodie's face scared her.

"Not forever, Broden!" Glynis rubbed his arm. "I will come back. Ye ken my son has the finest ship on the seas and will bring me safely home."

"No! I forbid it." Brodie dropped his head. "And now that I have said it, you will defy me all the more."

"I will not defy ye, Brodie. I love ye and it hurts my heart to think of leaving ye. I want yer permission to go. If Mum thinks Ross is needed at Glenhaven, 'tis bad. I need to see for myself and support my brother."

"We will all go then," Brodie answered.

"Ye canna and ye ken it." Glynis stared out over the rippling water. "I will take Aaron and leave Rory home with ye."

"Oh? We split our sons like Solomon in the Bible?" Brodie said through gritted teeth.

"Not in that way. Ye are exaggerating."

"Do I not have the right to exaggerate? My wife tells me she will take one son and go to Scotland to return some day. What if I said those words to you?"

"I would think it must be verra important for ye to leave the family."

"Was this your mother's idea? Did she say something on the walk to the house?"

"No! I have been thinking about it since the day she walked into

Heather's house. Do not fight me, Brodie. I canna go and ken yer angry with me."

"I will not fight you," Brodie whispered.

"What did ye say?"

"You may go, but only if Ross decides to return to Scotland, and I do not think he will."

Glynis laughed. "Ye are making a safe bet then?" She knelt behind him, rubbed his back and ran her hand into his auburn hair. "If I go, I will miss us." She breathed on his neck and placed a kiss. "And what we are to each other."

When Brodie turned to look at her, Glynis had slid her dress from her shoulders, exposing her bare skin to the waist. She saw the spark in Brodie's eyes which welled with tears and dropped to the blanket, her dark hair splayed about her. He lifted his shirt over his head and lay next to her.

"I cannot live without you." He breathed into her ear.

"Ye can and ye will. No jail time for ye. I will speak to Jock if I must." Glynis recalled the day she found Brodie in a cell, a broken shell of a man because she left with Aaron. "Ye have Rory now, Brodie. Dinna start drinking the whiskey again."

"I would never." Brodie's hands were on her dress, tugging it the rest of the way, over her hips and down her legs. He brought her close, their two hearts seemed to beat as one and he made love to her as he never had before.

———

"*I* see him!" Rory yelled. "Uncle Hiram!" He jumped from the porch and ran to meet the man on the horse.

"Rory!" Glynis called to him. "Take his horse to the barn."

"Aww!" Rory stomped over to where Hiram brought his steed to a halt.

"And dinna throw the saddle on the barn floor and say yer done," Glynis added.

After the morning in the woods, Brodie and Glynis had joined her mother on the front porch to wait for Hiram. They watched as he spoke with Rory, crouching down to his level and rising again, tousling the boy's hair. Hiram lifted his hand in greeting. Even from a distance, he appeared nervous.

"Hiram," Glynis said when he reached the bottom of the porch stairs. "I would like to introduce my mother, Fiona MacLaren."

Hiram walked up the three steps and paused in front of Fiona. He dipped at the waist and said, "It is a pleasure to finally meet you, Lady Fiona. Your servant." He took her hand and placed a light kiss on top. "I see where Glynis got her fine looks. Your daughter resembles you, my lady."

"Thank ye, Hiram. I am glad we finally meet. Your brother has been a guest at Glenhaven many a time. It was always a pleasure to have him. His friend?" Fiona pursed her lips. "Not as much."

"I am sorry John Alder caused your family so much grief. I hear he is happily married and living at Essex Estates in England."

"We thank the Lord He showed John the way," Fiona answered.

"To England, my lady?" Hiram smiled at Glynis and she chuckled.

"Aye, and much more." The corners of Fiona's mouth twitched.

"Please, Hiram, join us," Brodie said. "Unless you would like to rest before dinner?"

"I would like to join you." Hiram nodded and took a seat.

An uncomfortable silence followed. Glynis looked at Brodie with wide eyes, wondering what her mother thought of the Englishman in their midst. Even with all his schooling and noble background, Hiram was never the best at initiating conversation. Glynis had the sudden urge to check on dinner until her mother looked toward him and said, "Aaron told me the story of Gulliver's Travels. He said you brought the book as a gift for him and Rory."

"Yes, I did," Hiram answered a little too eagerly.

"What is your opinion of the Yahoos, Mr. Coward?" Fiona said with a lift of the eyebrow.

Glynis listened to his long-winded explanation of humans versus animals, peppered with questions from Fiona. Brodie's voice then entered the conversation, and she leaned back in her chair, content and satisfied.

CHAPTER 11

*J*uliet hummed as she prepared breakfast for the family excited by the news Edward Coward, her good friend, planned a visit to Gregor's Cove today. His brother, Hiram, had arrived the end of June and it took Edward almost four weeks to call on him. After breakfast, she planned to sit on the porch and wait for his arrival. He had to pass their house before heading to the Gregors.

"Ye are in a good mood, lass," Fiona said as she entered the kitchen. "What can I do to help ye?"

"I am almost done, Mother. We can have a cup of tea together."

"I will ready it while you finish." Fiona maneuvered around Juliet to get the hot water and tea caddy. "I thought ye'd have a fancy tea set," she said.

"I do not need those things. Ross has offered many times." Juliet put her hand on her hip. "I had hoped you'd know by now I do not need finer things to make me happy."

"I am sorry, lass. Ye are a good woman and mum." Fiona patted Juliet's face on the way to the table. "But I only have my memories from long ago."

Juliet suppressed a gasp. "You thought I was shallow and vain?"

"At times." Fiona winked. "We had different ways, Juliet. Sometimes yer way was best. I ken it now but back then ye seemed different."

"Thank you for changing your opinion." Juliet dipped her head.

"Tell me, why are ye so happy today?"

"I always am."

Fiona cocked her head. "Dinna try to fool an old woman. Sit with me, tea is ready."

"Well…" Juliet wondered how Fiona would react to the news. "Edward Coward is coming for a visit. Do you remember him? He is Hiram's brother."

"Aye, I do. The Sassenach, John Alder's friend." Fiona nodded her head. "Remember we have a constant reminder running through the castle."

Juliet smiled. "I could never forget Eva named her son after Edward. I hope it is not too much of a burden for Donnach to bear."

"Edward Coward is the only Sassenach Donnach ever liked."

"He liked Edward?" Juliet widened her eyes. *So after all these years, he still does not like me.*

"I should say he respected him, Juliet. We ken he left England hoping to protect ye. He thought if he came to America, John Alder would stay home where he belonged."

"I wish John would have stayed in England. I am sorry for the trouble I brought to the family."

"Och, no, lass. If not ye, then something else would have happened. Ye had no control over his grace, John Alder," Fiona said his name as if she had a bad taste in her mouth. "He has been gone from Scotland nine years, and we hope to never see the likes of him again."

"We feared John might show up in the colonies. Edward has kept his promise to never say he saw us here in New Jersey."

"In the early years, we waited for each letter from ye, hoping he stayed true to his word," Fiona replied. "After all this time, I feel Edward can be trusted."

Juliet laughed. "You sound like Ross."

Fiona chuckled. "He is most like me, Juliet. Donnach thinks he sees himself in Ross. 'Tis not true. Ross will kill for his family. For Glenhaven? Not as much."

"He would protect the clan, Fiona."

"I ken, but if given a choice he'd find another way than go to war." Fiona wrapped her hands around her teacup. "Now Duncan? He would fight to the end for the clan. Donnach does not see the burning in his son's eyes, the passion when he speaks of Glenhaven as I do. In a way…"

Juliet stared at her mother-in-law. "What?"

"He should be the next chief, laird of the land."

"Oh!"

"Ye didna hear it from me, lassie. If ye say I told ye, I will deny it." Fiona wiggled a finger at her.

"I will not betray your confidence, Mother. Is this the reason you came? You want Ross to return to Scotland to pacify Donnach but hope he will see Duncan for who he is?"

"I have two sons, Juliet. Both are precious to me. I want them to be happy. Ross is the eldest so by rights is the heir. Duncan is resigned to it and will find his way."

Juliet sipped her tea and studied Fiona. She had her opinions and kept them to herself all those years ago yet felt comfortable sharing in her company now. Juliet remembered many days sitting in Fiona's parlor, sewing and mending, while Fiona spoke against the English and proudly told the history of the Scottish clans. Sometimes Juliet had cringed when she heard what British soldiers did to their people. In the colonies, the redcoat presence was felt but not as strongly. The family paid their taxes to the English government and heard grumblings from people in town over the amount, but no soldiers rode through Gregor's Cove looking for certain clans or people who'd committed a crime against the crown like in Scotland. For the little time Juliet spent in Glenhaven, she'd learned about the suffocating hand of their ruler, King George.

A year ago, King George had died of a stroke. He was succeeded by his son, George II. Juliet knew little of this new king's reign. She'd hope he did not send another young, unsuspecting girl to wed someone for the good of the country even though her marriage was filled with love and happiness. She remembered the day she had to leave her father's estate in England, scared yet determined not to show it. John Alder had fought for her to stay, doing what he could at the time. He later discovered her father owed a large sum to the king and had used Juliet as collateral. Her father, the Duke of Norchester, Lord William Kingston brokered a deal with the king. If he could not pay his debt in time, Juliet could be offered to a Scottish laird, marry him or one of his sons to keep the peace between the two countries. He would not interfere or protest the transaction. She found it almost humorous that her marriage had not prevented conflict between the countries. Harmony did not last long, and Ross had joined the Uprising of Fifteen six months after their wedding.

"My dear," Fiona said, placing her hand on Juliet's arm. "You are lost in thought?"

"Oh!" Juliet started. "I am sorry. Yes, when I speak of Edward and John it brings up old memories. Some of them are good." Juliet smiled. "The ones before I left my father's estate, I keep close to my heart. Edward was an old friend, and John was someone I thought I loved."

"And do you still?"

"What?" Juliet widened her eyes. "Certainly not. I discovered what type of man John was when he took me from Glenhaven. Controlling and cruel. If I had stayed in England, I would have learned about the man too late and led a miserable life."

"Yer life with us is not as bad?" Fiona lifted the MacLaren eyebrow.

"Most of the time, no." Juliet gave her mother-in-law a smile and stood. "If you will excuse me, I will get our breakfast."

Lizbeth and Alec burst in the room, talking and laughing.

"If we go to the stream, we will find Cowan and Gwen," Lizbeth said with a giggle. "Kissing!"

"I do not want to see such a sight." Alec teased. "After my chores we will choose another place to ride."

"I want to look for the monster in the woods," Lizbeth begged. "Rory swears it is real."

"Yet, Aaron feels it's a ghost." Alec wiggled his fingers. "Do you want the creature to take you away?"

"No!" Lizbeth covered her eyes. "Mummy, make him stop."

"Now, Lizbeth." Fiona pulled the girl's hands away from her face. "Ye asked yer brother to take ye. Let me tell ye a secret. If ye were back in Scotland ye could hunt for the faeries."

"Ooh! I would like that, Granny. Would you come with me?"

"Of course."

"After breakfast will you tell me more about the faeries?"

"Your granny has many stories about them," Juliet said. "I heard she thought they had something to do with your Aunt Glynis and father being born a year apart in the same month of October."

"Och, Juliet! 'Tis true." Fiona waved her hand and laughed. "When they were bairns, I swore the faeries spoke to them and made them misbehave."

Everyone at the table laughed as Ross came through the entryway. "Good morning to ye." He nodded. "I see everyone is in a fine mood."

"At your expense, Da," Alec said, making everyone laugh again.

"Granny," Lizbeth said. "Da and Auntie were born in October. Is there something special about the month? Why did the faeries not speak to your other children?"

"In our world, October is a special month, my wee one. I will tell ye of Samhain and more later."

After breakfast, the men headed for the barn and Fiona helped Juliet straighten the kitchen. "I can finish, lass. Ye want to watch for Edward. Go. 'Tis quite all right. After Lizbeth and I wash the dishes, I will take her for a walk and tell her stories."

"Thank you, Fiona." Juliet took her by the hands. "I am glad we have gotten to know each other. I wish we could bring the rest of the family here and live out our days peacefully. Things are not good in Scotland, are they?"

"No," Fiona whispered. "I have spoken to Ross and told him the feelings of the people. I fear we will always be at war with the English, either in battle or in our minds."

"When will it stop?" Juliet cried, rubbing between her eyes to ease the tension in her head.

"'Tis a verra good question. After the Nineteen, the men have met in the shadows to discuss the Jacobite cause. Money is quietly being raised. The rumor is the Jacobites are stockpiling weapons in secret places."

"You have written about the Nineteen, as you call it, but it did not seem to have an impact as the Uprising did."

"'Twas a small rising, daughter. England and France had been at peace so the Jacobites found a new ally in Spain. Tensions were high between Spain and England during the time over a treaty they had signed." Fiona paused. "Highlanders did not join the cause as was thought and the Spanish fleet did not arrive to help, so the Jacobites who chose to engage in war were easily defeated."

"Do you think something will happen again? Another uprising?"

"Perhaps." Fiona's green eyes met Juliet's blue ones. "It could be a matter of time."

"Oh! I hope not." Juliet shook her head. "Or at least not in our lifetime."

"I hope yer right, daughter." Fiona patted Juliet's cheek. "Go now. Before ye miss yer friend."

Juliet caught sight of Edward when she stepped onto the front porch. Tall in the saddle, she recognized his stance and the way he rode the horse. She ran to the edge of the yard and waved. The horse picked up speed, dust clouds forming around its hooves. As Edward drew closer, he removed his tricorn hat from his head to expose his short brown hair. "Are you all right, Juliet?" His face wore a look of concern.

Edward dismounted, tied the horse to the hitching post by the trough and rushed toward her. He unbuttoned his regimental red coat, fashioned to fit his well-built frame and exposed a white shirt tucked into white leggings. His black boots were worn and dusty from the ride.

"Yes, Edward, I am fine." Juliet looked into his kind, brown eyes. "I knew you would come this way to visit your brother and hoped to see you. Would you like something to eat or drink after your journey?"

"I am fine. I brought drink with me and I fear the horse needs water more than I. It is turning into quite the warm day." Edward approached, took Juliet's hand and bowed over it with a kiss. "It is good to see you."

"We do not see each other as often as I'd like," Juliet answered. "Penelope insisted on staying in Boston and she and Hiram did not visit often which also kept you away. Come," Juliet put her arm through his. "Let us walk in the shade and you can tell me what is happening in New York City." She guided him toward the backyard.

Edward chuckled. "I pay little attention to what the upper class is doing, if that is what you mean."

"I find it hard to believe you are not invited to social gatherings, Edward. A handsome man such as yourself and unmarried?" Juliet narrowed her eyes. "You are not accepting the invitations, are you?"

"Do not accuse me of what you do not know." Edward teased. "I attend some parties. There is always a general's daughter or baron's niece someone wants me to meet."

"Do you still pine for the woman you left behind in England? You were courting a lady-in-waiting at the castle, I believe."

"Anna was a duke's daughter. I heard she married well." Edward paused under the shade of a tree. "She was lovely but not the woman I longed to marry."

"So…there was someone?"

"Yes…you."

Shocked by the admission, Juliet's hand flew to her mouth. "I did not know."

"I am aware."

"Would you like to sit?" Juliet gestured to the benches farther back in the yard trying to control her nerves. Her heart pounded as she led the way. *Will he tell me more? I never felt he was more than a friend. Before John came into my life, I could have fallen in love with Edward. I was so young and being three years older perhaps he was waiting for me to grow up?*

"After all these years, you are wondering why I am telling you now." Edward's chiseled jaw twitched as they sat together on the bench. "I did not want you to carry the guilt any longer. You thought I left England and the woman I loved with regrets. I may have married Anna if I had stayed, I will never know. If I had really loved her, I should have wed her and brought her to the colonies. As you see, I did not. I told you and Ross I was looking for adventure, to leave John's command and lead a regiment of my own. I meant it. I have found all of those things in the colonies."

"But not someone to love," Juliet whispered.

"By choice, Juliet," Edward answered. "Remember our walks in your father's garden?"

"How could I forget?"

"William loved to grow roses and named a rosebush after you. If I recall, he called you his English Rose." Edward smiled.

"Until I was not. He easily sold me to the highest bidder." Juliet dropped her head. "I am sorry. It sounds harsh and I do not mean it to be. Father has apologized and thought he could get the money in time to pay his debt."

"It was a cruel thing, Juliet, yet you are happy. Yes?"

"Oh, yes, Edward. So much so. I have three children and a loving husband. Our life in Gregor's Cove has been wonderful except for the occasional sadness. Did you hear Angus Forbes died in a fire?"

"I did. I am sorry he is gone. Forbes was an exceptional man and blacksmith."

Juliet wiped a tear trickling down her cheek. "He was."

"His wife, Nell? I heard she lost two children. It must have been hard."

"Yes, she moved back to Sexton Estates to live. She was told she'd always have a home there."

"Interesting." Edward tapped his lips. "Oh, and speaking of interesting, I have news to tell. As you are aware, John married Lady Camilla Grey, the Earl of Kent's daughter. They recently had a child, a girl they named Abigail."

"After his sister? How wonderful!" Juliet recalled the closeness of the two siblings. John had been devastated when Abigail passed away. "She was so young when she died."

"He'd always hoped I would marry his sister," Edward replied. "It is the reason I brought him to Norchester for a visit. I wanted him to meet you and tell him I planned to court you so he would drop the idea.

Instead…" He inhaled deeply then slowly let the air out through puckered lips. "He thought I wanted him to meet you and see if there was interest. John was witty and charming as always and you only had eyes for him during our visit. I sometimes regret bringing him to Norchester. He wasted no time asking your father if he might court you."

"Why did you not tell me, Edward?"

"John made it known when we left your home, he would marry you one day and no man had better stand in his way. Remember I was the second son of a duke, but he would become the Duke of Essex one day."

Juliet shivered. "I am glad he found someone to marry and now has a family."

"I am sorry for reminding you of a sad time in your life. I wanted you to understand I left for more than one reason. Yes, I had to remove myself from a dire situation, John was too dependent on me and I could not go on seeing you hurt any longer. But I did this for myself. I wanted to start over in a new place. When my orders came and said I would be stationed in New York City, I felt destiny intervened. I would be close to my brother and have an opportunity to have my own regiment far from England where no one knew me."

"Oh Edward! When we came to the colonies, we were quite thoughtless. Our family asked you to make promises we never should have. We begged you keep our whereabouts secret from John. We are grateful to you and what you have done, but I felt you were angry with me at the time and maybe still are."

"Never."

"Are you sure? After you sent the message to ask for no more favors, we did not see you again until Hiram's wedding."

"I needed time, Juliet. I swore to protect you from John and I always will, but I could not visit you or look into your lovely sapphire eyes and see friendship not love. I had to come to terms with the fact we are friends and nothing more."

"Oh, Edward, I am sorry if I hurt you or caused you harm in any way. I am glad you feel we can be friends. When we spoke at the wedding, you assured me things were fine, but I have always wondered if you meant those words. Ten years have gone by quickly, and you were hardly a part of them."

"I am back now. Hiram will visit Glynis each summer and I will come as often as I can."

"Do you promise?"

"For you? Anything."

CHAPTER 12

"*H*iram, quit yer pacing. Edward will be here soon." Glynis checked the rooms of the house one more time. She wanted everything in place before their esteemed guest arrived.

"I am sorry if I am disturbing you, Glynis." Hiram folded his hands at his waist. "I saw Edward a month ago before I boarded the ferry to Perth Amboy. He appeared troubled but insisted he was fine. Do you think he is ill?"

"No, I dinna. Edward could be in love." Glynis lifted her brows. "It may be too soon to announce his intentions."

"Oh, I do hope you are right." Hiram motioned for Glynis to come closer. "May I tell you something in confidence?"

"Aye, ye can trust me."

"In most of the colonies, the military rank and file is filled with common laborers and low-quality soldiers. Edward has had to deal with insubordination from criminals and the dregs of society. In Massachusetts the militia is made up of men who have been skilled artisans or had a middle-class upbringing. More palatable, do you not think? As a member of the governor's council, I would like to recommend Edward for a position in Boston. Of course, it will be comparable or better than the one he holds now."

"Did Edward ask ye to help him move to Boston?" Glynis squinted at him. "Or are ye meddling in his life?"

"If you have to put it so harshly, no he did not, and yes, I am meddling. I would like my brother to live closer to me."

Glynis made a noise in her throat. "And ye being the eldest ken he will oblige."

"I will let Edward choose but would give anything for him to come to Boston. Besides, it is time I did something for him. As the eldest, I should have been the protector of my brothers, but often time, the roles were reversed. There is no denying Edward is a handsome man, strong and sturdy." Hiram hung his head. "We are not the same."

"Ye have good qualities, Hiram, which make ye special. Ye dinna need muscles to prove yer a man or a bonny face to win a lass. Rory and Aaron think yer the best, they canna wait for ye to visit. There is a kindness to ye," Glynis said. "Some men never have a good word for anyone. Ye try to see the best in people."

"Those are kind words, Glynis. Thank you. But I have lost so much." Hiram gave her a look which made her feel his pain. "Will you help me?"

"Ye ken I will, Hiram. Promise me ye willna use Penelope as a reason for Edward to join ye in Boston. Speak of the work, how he will bring value to the new position."

"He would not have to look for housing, although the general has been adamant about the people of the city opening their homes to his soldiers. Edward can live with me."

"Ye have it all planned. Edward will be thrilled." Glynis rolled her eyes. Even though she felt sorry for him and wanted to help, Hiram did not hear what she said. She could only hope the conversation with his brother went well.

"Will you wait with me, Glynis? I will carry the tea tray outside if you will get the door."

"Isna it beneath ye to carry a tray?" She teased.

"Not in the country." Hiram grinned. "You have taught me well. Every man for himself." He chuckled. "It is a good thing my mother cannot see me. I see her swooning at the thought of me doing servants' work."

"She'd swoon over her eldest son doing chores?" Glynis held the door open for him. "My lads ken how to do every chore just as Brodie's mum taught him. It has served him well."

"Perhaps it has. I am learning to fend for myself like when you taught me to fight."

Glynis let out a delightful laugh. "Behind the crates on the Pembroke, I remember. Ye were a willing learner, and it has saved ye often."

"Yes, many think I am an easy target but find out otherwise." Hiram smiled. "I miss the days on the ship and your company."

"Much has changed since then, hasna it?" A feeling of melancholy swept over Glynis. "The time on the Pembroke can feel like it happened yesterday and sometimes is a far distant thought."

"I know what you mean." Hiram set the tray on the table between them.

"I will pour, Hiram. Dinna use all yer helpfulness in one day."

"Thank you." Hiram smiled when she handed him a cup. "I am glad I have one more month before I return to Boston. I'd forgotten how invigorating it can be here."

Glynis held her tongue. She wished to blame Penelope, but Hiram would defend his wife. Besides, the woman had passed away, and her mother said not to speak ill of the dead or they would visit during Samhain when the veil between the world and the otherworld was thin. Glynis shuddered at the thought of coming face to face with Penelope.

"Oh! I think I see him." Hiram stood and cupped his hand over his round glasses. "Edward!" He waved and walked down the steps to greet him.

The men chatted while Edward tended his horse, then Hiram brought him to the porch.

"Glynis," Edward said with a bow. "A pleasure to see you as always."

"'Tis good to see you, too, Edward. Please sit. How was your trip?"

"Edward said he would have been earlier but stopped to see Juliet," Hiram said. "She was also waiting on her porch."

Glynis stared at Hiram as if to say, "Let the man speak." "Did he now? How is my brother's wife, Edward?"

109

"She is fine." Edward sat and accepted the tea. "Thank you. I can stay overnight but need to return to my regiment tomorrow. The weather has been good, and the ferry is running so I do not foresee a problem."

"Is there trouble in your regiment again?" Hiram asked. "You deserve better than those ruffians who cannot follow an order. In fact..." He tapped his chin as if he had a thought. "You should come to Boston."

"To visit?"

"No, to live."

A strained silence fell over them. Glynis shifted in her seat, pretended to sip her tea and looked at Hiram over the edge of the cup.

"Unless you do not want to live in Boston," Hiram finally said.

"And if I come, what would I do, brother?"

"I could find you a suitable position."

"I like living in New York. I am close to Amboy and can visit you here."

"True, but you could live in my house, dine with me nightly and I could purchase a highly regarded position for you in the army."

"I am afraid I have to turn down your kind offer, brother."

"Please, Edward, think about it."

Glynis felt Hiram got his answer but would continue badgering his brother if she didn't intervene. "Is there any summer illness in New York, Edward? Have most of the upper class gone to cooler destinations or did some stay in the city? If so, do they still hold parties?" She stopped, realizing she rambled.

"Many leave for the reasons you have given, Glynis. We have been lucky so far. Not too many sick and not so many parties." Edward chuckled.

Glynis rose, gathered the teacups and placed everything on the tray. "Hiram, why dinna ye and Edward take a walk in the woods and look for Rory's monster? I am sure he would love to hear about this mystery man on our land."

"A monster? Why did you not say? I am up for a good hunt, Hiram. Lead the way."

"If ye find him, Edward, make sure ye tie him up good. Rory will never forgive ye if ye let him get away."

"I would not want to disappoint the boy so I will try my best," Edward said with a wave of hand as the men left the porch.

Glynis smiled as she watched the brothers head to the back of the house, hoping they'd find time to bond in the forest and alleviate some of Hiram's long hidden pain.

———

*J*uliet nervously paced in the yard. *Do I tell Ross what Edward said? He cares for me, loves me? I cannot. The feuding will never end. Ross has come to terms with Hiram and Edward. He finally trusts them. This will bring up old wounds. Ross may fear Edward will turn into another John. Oh! Why did he tell me this news?* She sank onto the bench and stared at the house.

The back door opened, and Lizbeth came bounding out and skipped through the grass until she reached Juliet. "Mummy! I learned about Scottish faeries today. Granny told me so many stories I need to write them down. I could make a book and draw pictures of them. Would it not be wonderful?"

"It sounds delightful, my darling, and will fill your days until school begins."

"Granny sent me out to remind you it is Wednesday."

"I am fully aware the day is… Oh! *Wednesday.*"

"Yes." Lizbeth nodded. "The day Cowan brings Gwen to dinner. You have nothing started and did not discuss the meal plan with Granny." Lizbeth crossed her arms. "Are you all right, Mummy? You have a faraway look in your eyes as if you are not paying attention to me."

"I am giving you my full attention, Lizbeth." Juliet smiled. "It is warm, and I need a cool drink."

"Does Gwen know about faeries? She was eleven when she came to America from Scotland, so I hope she does! Maybe she even met one. Can faeries stow away on ships? It is the only way they could come to America." Lizbeth sat next to Juliet and rested her head on her mother's shoulder. "Granny said faeries are sensitive beings and can easily have their feelings hurt. Is that why they cause mischief?"

"Perhaps." Juliet's knowledge of Scottish folklore was mediocre at best, yet she'd heard of many kinds of faeries, good and bad.

"Mum, have you heard of a changeling? I think it is quite awful. Faeries can kidnap a baby and replace it with one of their own. I would never want to be kidnapped."

"I prefer the benevolent house faerie, the Brownie," Juliet said. "He picks a house and helps the woman with chores. I have heard it said he has been brought to America by the Scots."

"Really?" Lizbeth looked at her with eyes of wonder. "Did they sneak on board the ships?"

"Or hid in the family's trunks." Juliet poked Lizbeth in the side. "Do you think we have one living with us?"

"I will have to ask Granny." Lizbeth laughed.

"Speaking of Granny, we best go inside and help her."

Lizbeth ran ahead of her to the house. Juliet slowed her pace, took one more look around the grounds and made a promise to keep Edward's conversation to herself. When she stepped through the entryway Fiona was in the kitchen tending to the pot hanging over the fire. "Did ye have a good chat with yer countryman?" she asked without looking up from her duties.

"Yes," Juliet said, trying not to sound as if she lied. *It was most disturbing, but I will put the thoughts away with my past life.* "Lizbeth and I will set the table in the dining room. Cowan and Gwen should be here soon."

"Mum thinks we have a Brownie living with us, Granny," Lizbeth said, and Juliet was grateful for the change of subject.

"Och, I think the Brownie is me." Fiona glanced up, lifting an eyebrow, and they laughed. "The pork and potatoes will be ready soon."

"Thank you for starting the meal, Fiona. I made a fresh loaf of bread this morning," Juliet said. "Lizbeth, please put the jam on the table."

Ross entered the back door, wiped his brow and kissed Juliet on the cheek on his way to the bucket in the corner to wash. "I saw Cowan and Gwen on the road. They will be here in a minute or so."

"Have you seen Alec?" Juliet asked.

"The lad canna stay away from the forge. He is determined to get a new sword since he lost his in the fire. I told Jamie not to indulge him and work on it when he had time. Alec kens 'tis Wednesday and should come home for dinner."

"Good. We will have all the family at the table." Juliet nodded and went to the dining room to set out the dishes and ready it for guests.

---

*E*xcept to grow taller, Gwen had not changed in looks since the first day Juliet met her on the ship. A plain-looking girl with ordinary brown eyes and pale skin, her height almost matched Cowan's. Juliet decided Gwen must take after her father who'd been killed in the 1715 Uprising. Sophie, her mother, always fussed over her, putting ribbons in her straight hair which would not hold a curl and bought the latest fashions once she married Jasper. Juliet always wondered if Sophie thought it helped to make her daughter look more beautiful.

"Mum! We are here," Cowan called when he spotted her in the dining room.

"May I be of any help?" Gwen untied her bonnet and removed her expensive gloves, placing them inside the hat.

Cowan took her accessories and set them on a table by the front door. "Anything I can do, Mum?"

"Yes, tell the others you are here." Juliet straightened and smiled at the couple. "Good day to you, Gwen. Is that a new dress?"

"Aye, Mum insisted." Gwen gingerly touched the skirt. "I feel 'tis too fancy for this time of day." The rose silk fabric had embroidered flowers around the waist, and Gwen wore matching rose and green ribbons in her hair.

"It is lovely." Juliet quietly agreed.

"Do ye think?" she asked, gazing at the floor.

"Yes, Gwen, you look lovely as always."

"Gwen and Cowan are here!" Lizbeth shouted, rushing from the kitchen. "Gwen," she said taking the woman's hand. "Granny told me of the faeries. Did you ever meet one? Do you have any stories? I am going to write a book."

"My, 'tis quite an undertaking but I am proud of ye for wanting to write a book."

"You are a teacher, Gwen. Perhaps you can help me." Lizbeth slipped her hand into Gwen's and said to Cowan and Juliet, "We will be in the parlor if you need us."

Cowan chuckled as he took the plates from Juliet and slid them onto the table. "Ye dinna have to worry, Mum."

"I am not worried." Juliet followed him placing the silverware. "But Gwen has lived at the manor for ten years."

"She hasna changed, Mum. Gwen is still the same girl we met on the Pembroke. 'Twas her mother who hoped for a good marriage once she arrived in America. Sophie dinna want to become an indentured servant, and dare I say she must have found white heather before we crossed because her prayers were answered."

Juliet wrinkled her brow. "White heather? How would it help her?"

"I forget ye dinna ken all our customs, Mum. Scots have passed the tale down through generations." Cowan paused while he finished setting the table. When he completed his task, he looked at Juliet and said, "Malvina, daughter of the third century warrior, Ossian, lost her lover in battle. Her tears dripped onto the purple heather of the Highlands, changing them to white. When she saw what happened she declared, 'Although it is the symbol of my sorrow, may the white heather bring good fortune to all who find it.' White heather is rarer than purple, and when a person finds the flower, we believe it can bring good luck."

"Then I agree. Sophie fell into a patch of white heather." Juliet suppressed a giggle.

Cowan grinned and nodded. "Aye." His expression changed to a serious one. "Gwen doesna want what her mother has. She wishes to be free of that life, fill her own with happiness and adventure."

"She sounds like your Aunt Glynis. Although the poor girl did not have the same freedoms as Glynis. Your aunt has realized she did many things at Glenhaven which other parents would not have allowed. She was given freedom and is grateful."

"I always wondered why Donnach didna find a match for her."

"He may have feared she'd run the suitor through with her dirk when he was not looking." Juliet covered her mouth. "I am sorry. Do not repeat my words, Cowan."

"I willna, Mum, but ye seem in good spirits."

"I always am," Juliet said and playfully swatted at him with a cloth napkin.

"I mean extra happy." Cowan held up one hand to protect himself while grabbing his own cloth.

"What is going on in here?" Ross asked. "I expected dinner, not my wife and son in a napkin fight."

Juliet burst into laughter. "Oh, Ross, we were having a serious discussion and somehow it turned into this."

"Then, I am glad it did." Ross wrapped his arm around Juliet's waist. "Mum asked me to retrieve ye. She wants to ken if the food should be served."

"Has Alec returned home?"

"Aye, he came in through the back. We are all here." Ross looked at Cowan. "Ye brought Gwen?"

"She is in the parlor with Lizbeth helping her write a book."

"A book?" Ross raised his brow. "It appears I have missed much in the few minutes I was in the kitchen."

"Ross," Juliet said. "Lizbeth is excited about it. Do not ruin her fun."

"I wouldna. What is the book about?"

"Faeries."

Ross rubbed his chin. "I may have some stories to pass along."

"No!" Juliet and Cowan said together, glanced at each other and laughed.

"Why not?"

"You tend to…" Juliet looked at Cowan for support.

"Have too much knowledge, Da. Let Lizbeth write bairns' tales."

"Fine, I will only help if asked. Juliet, I'll be in the kitchen. Dinna take too long."

"I will finish the silverware and come," Juliet answered.

"'Twas a close call, Mum. I thought ye would tell him what Auntie Glynis always says. It takes Da an hour to tell a five-minute story." He chuckled.

"Do not get me started laughing again, son." Juliet placed her hand on his chest and felt his strong muscles, reminding her of the man he'd become. "Bring your guest to the table and I will go to the kitchen."

"Thank ye for doing this, Mum."

Juliet looked at him with quizzical eyes.

"Wednesday dinners."

"Oh! It is nothing, Cowan. We love you and want what is best." *Even if it is Gwen.*

CHAPTER 13

*L*ast-minute tasks of sewing and visiting the general store in Perth Amboy filled the days leading up to the Sexton anniversary party. Once she heard about the festive occasion, Fiona insisted on paying for the women's dresses. Silks, satin and lace had been ordered, a seamstress hired, and work had begun on the gowns by the end of June. Fine silk gloves and hats came from Boston to Hans Vogel's general store for the gala. Women had flocked to his shop, buying out his inventory in a few days.

For the breakfast and into the afternoon, the MacLaren women would wear formal daywear, the popular mantua, which had an unboned loose-fitting bodice. A robe with a train was draped up to the hips and pulled back to expose a contrasting petticoat. Juliet had chosen a pale blue floral for her robe while Heather would wear an abstract pattern of gold and green. Glynis insisted on the MacLaren green and blue in bold stripes and Fiona surprisingly chose rose silk with gold thread. Each wore a petticoat to match one of the colors in their main dress. The women would then don their finest satin before dinner. As stated in the invitation, the Sextons would provide a place for women to rest, change and refresh themselves.

The men brought out their finest Glengarry bonnets for dress while ones were made for the younger MacLaren male offspring. The dark caps of thick-milled woolen material were decorated with a pom on top and had a band of red, black and white check around the lower edge. Two black ribbons, fashioned in an upside-down V, hung down the back. The men would forgo wearing kilts in deference to Jamie who could not display his colors. They'd still look splendid in velvet coats of rust, green, blue or black with white ruffled shirts, silk vests and matching knickers. To finish the look, they'd pair their outfits with white or black silk stockings and fine leather shoes.

The day of the party, the family carried boxes out to the wagons filled with attire for everyone except the children. They would dress in their best clothes and wear them throughout the day. Ross hoped they had everything they needed as he examined the wagon and finally gave the command to leave.

Two wagons rolled up to the front entrance of Jasper Sexton's manor within the hour. The MacLaren family plus Hiram were helped to the ground by house slaves dressed in fine green silk waistcoats and white ruffled shirts. Their black silk breeches had been tucked inside leather boots making the procession of men look as if ready to receive the king himself.

The festivities began with the formal breakfast inside the manor. The family was escorted up the wide front staircase leading to the open double doors of the mansion where Jasper and Sophie stood in the grand foyer greeting guests.

"Hiram, my man." Jasper placed his hand on Hiram's shoulder and shook hands with the other.

"Why is he acting as if Hiram is his best friend?" Glynis whispered to Ross.

"He was in the wedding if I recall," Ross said under his breath as they inched toward the hosts.

"Ross and Juliet," Sophie breathed in their names and exhaled when they reached her. "It has been too long." She touched Juliet's arm.

"Good day and congratulations on the tenth anniversary of yer wedding." Ross bowed to her and shook Jasper's hand. "Yer corn and wheat are doing well?"

"More than well, Ross. An excellent year. When Father returns to England he will speak with the brokers. We should be able to ship a bountiful crop across the sea besides what is sold here. Yes, indeed. A wonderful year." Jasper looked at Ross with cold, calculating eyes.

Ross had seen him on many occasions visiting a tavern or a widow's home on trips to town. Yet, an unspoken gentleman's agreement kept him silent.

"And I have the pleasure of finally meeting your mother, Lady Fiona MacLaren," Jasper said and bent at the waist. "Good morning to you, my lady. Your servant." He took Fiona's gloved hand and kissed the top.

"'Tis a pleasure, Mr. Sexton." Fiona nodded. "Congratulations on yer anniversary."

"Thank you," Jasper answered and looked at Ross. "Your mother is quite the beauty. Glynis favors her."

"Verra kind of ye to say, Jasper." Ross longed to get away before Glynis, who stood behind him in line, scratched the man's eyes out. He heard her grumbling and turned to Juliet. "Should we find our seats?"

The family said their proper well wishes and were shown to the dining room.

"Can we get the day started so we can go home," Ross whispered to his wife.

Juliet tapped his arm with her fan. "Ross, we have just arrived." She leaned in closer. "And, I agree." As they walked to their table, she said, "Sophie told me Jasper balked at the idea of inviting children, but after she explained their sons needed to meet those in their social status, he agreed."

"The lads have only played with the indentured servants' bairns, and due to their ages, I doubt Jasper lets them anymore."

"Yes, Sophie feels Jonathan and Henry should be exposed to children their age and similar rank. She told me she had the drawing room prepared as a separate place for the children to eat breakfast away from the adults to appease Jasper and afterward they will be taken outside for games."

"Servants took Lizbeth to this room?"

"Yes, after I gave permission, although I doubt we had a choice.

Lizbeth went with Heather's three and Glynis' two, so she is not alone. Alec and Cowan are old enough to dine with us."

Once they chose a table, Ross pulled out a chair for his mother and helped her get seated. He turned to Juliet and offered the same assistance. Alec, Cowan and Gwen took the three chairs next to Juliet. Ross' sisters and husbands sat across from them.

Tall, elegant silver candelabras held white tapered candles and were surrounded by crystal bowls filled with white hydrangeas, the focal point of every table. Fine sterling silver pots of coffee, tea and chocolate ran down the center of the shiny mahogany tables. Sugar bowls and cream pots were nestled among them. The manservants, dressed in crisp white shirts, black velvet pants and black stockings with leather shoes, carried silver platters of rolls and sweet cakes into the room. Another line of servants appeared with steaks and pork chops still sizzling from the griddle and a variety of fricassees, beef or chicken mixed with vegetables. The aroma of fine herbs and spices hung in the air. Everyone ate from Chinese blue and white porcelain plates and drank from silver cups and crystal goblets.

Polite conversation was made during the meal, and when guests finished, they were invited to sit on the veranda to watch the children's games and enjoy the weather while sipping claret from tiny crystal goblets. When Ross and Juliet stepped onto the veranda, he noticed a trio of men setting up in the corner to play music.

Lizbeth spotted her parents and waved her hand. Her cheeks were flushed pink, and she appeared to be having a good time. She skipped toward them, looking happy and excited.

"Da, Mummy, guess what?"

"What?" Ross asked.

"Jonathan Sexton poured my tea! He asked if I would like cream and sugar and I said yes. He has requested me to be his partner in the sack race. Will you watch?"

"Of course, we would not miss it. We will not move from this spot," Juliet answered.

"Mummy, all the girls got a wooden tea caddy to start our collection. The box is beautiful with a hand-carved top, and there is room inside for the accoutrements. When I opened the caddy, there were four silver teaspoons inside." Lizbeth bounced to where Fiona sat. "We can have a tea party, Granny, when I get home. Will you please hold it for me?"

"Of course." Fiona patted her face. "I will guard it with my life."

"Well," Lizbeth said with a laugh. "You may not have to but thank you."

"What about the lads, Lizbeth? Did they get gifts?" Ross was curious.

"They got a horse and rider made from metal. It's Henry or Jonathan's favorite toy. I forget." Lizbeth shrugged and wrinkled her nose. "I do not know which boy likes it, but the toy is quite handsome." She pointed to the musical trio. "Are you going to dance with Mummy, Da?"

"I certainly will, and I also plan to dance with another bonny lass."

"Oh!" Lizbeth's eyes widened. "Will Mum be jealous?"

"Not if she sees me dancing with ye." Ross winked. "Now go play. Have fun and win the race." He reached for Juliet's hand and squeezed. "'Tis better than I thought 'twould be. Dancing and dinner."

"The brandy is being poured, Ross. Perhaps you would like a glass?"

"And would ye like a glass of sweet wine?" Ross stood, waving to Jamie and Brodie.

"Yes, thank you, Ross."

"Mum?"

"I am fine as I am, Ross. I want to keep a clear head today." Fiona closed one eye and whispered. "Jasper Sexton is clever as a fox. We need to watch him."

As Ross walked with his brothers-in-law to the refreshment table, he mulled over what his mother said. He did not see a threat, yet she did. "What do ye think, Jamie? Ye ken Mum better than Brodie. Does she have a reason to worry about Sexton?"

"Och, no, Ross. She is getting used to our ways here in America. We've lived with the man ten years and nothing has happened. Living with Donnach, makes ye distrustful."

"Aye, it can." Ross held up his glass in a toast. "To Donnach."

Brodie and Jamie repeated the same, and they drank to the bottom of their glasses.

---

*J*asper Sexton's father, Craig, had Nell Forbes on his arm since breakfast. His singular attention caught Juliet's eye. "Ross." She nudged him while standing at the sweets table. "Do you think it is an odd pairing?"

"Who, my love?"

"Craig Sexton and Nell. She lost her husband two months ago and should be in mourning."

"She wears black." Ross nodded at the young widow. "But still is a bonny lass." He cleared his throat. "Yet doesna compare to ye."

"I am not asking for compliments, Ross." Juliet chuckled and said under her breath, "I believe they are coming our way."

"Ross and Juliet," Craig said with a bow. "I do not believe we have had the privilege of speaking today. Annella insisted we join you."

Annella?

As if she read Juliet's mind, Nell said, "Craig prefers my full name. He says it rolls off the tongue like a song."

Craig gave a hearty laugh. "Is she not delightful?" He smiled at Nell, and Juliet realized he'd fallen for her. Despite having four children, Nell had a youthful appearance and figure, her creamy complexion complementing her ginger color hair.

"Mr. Sexton, I am not a delight. I am a woman in mourning," Nell replied in a soft tone.

"You have done an admirable job keeping up your spirits, Annella." He looked at Juliet. "Her children are her priority, yet she finds time to come to the house and read to me."

"What a kind service you provide," Juliet said.

Nell stared at the ground. "Yes, at his request."

Nell had always been good at sending Juliet signals. Craig was more smitten with Nell than she was with him and he looked for excuses to be near her. Reading had been his idea.

"I keep insisting she move to the main house," Craig continued.

"Jasper has more than enough rooms. Why live in an indentured servant's home when she could have the best of everything?"

"Norris is my brother-in-law, Mr. Sexton. I lived there before I married Angus, and I was told by my sister I would always have a home there."

"Quite kind of Norris to abide by his wife's wishes, but surely since your sister…"

"Father?" Jasper approached. "May I have a word?"

"Certainly." Craig bent at the waist. "If you will excuse me?"

"Aye, we will," Ross said with a nod of the head.

"Annella, I will leave you in their capable hands until I return."

Nell rolled her eyes as they watched him walk away with his son. "Even since he arrived, he thinks he owns me." She looked at Juliet. "I am not an indentured servant. I can leave here any time I want."

"Is Craig aware of it?" Juliet asked.

"Aye, I have told him many times. He doesna seem to hear." Nell slipped her arm through Juliet's. "Walk with me?"

Juliet looked to Ross. "Go. I will be here," he said.

The women headed to the gardens where they could stroll the paths and not be overheard.

After admiring the trees and flowers, Nell stopped when they arrived at a bench. "Please, sit, Juliet. I have much to tell you and most is not good news." She lowered her body onto the seat with a sigh. "Things are quite different at Sexton Estates from how I remember them."

"You have been gone ten years, I expect much has changed."

"'Tis not what I mean." Nell looked at Juliet with tears in her eyes. "When I first came with the others, there was so much hope. People were eager to work off their contracts so one day they could start a new life in this land." She pulled a handkerchief from inside her glove and dabbed the outside corner of her eye. "The ones bound to Jasper Sexton are treated no better than livestock…and the slaves worse. Small infractions receive major penalties. There are so many rules 'tis easy to break them. If someone even dreams of escaping…" She put her hand to her heart. "I canna say what happens." Nell dropped her head and studied her hands.

Juliet swallowed the lump growing in her throat, not surprised by the news, but said, "I'd heard Jasper is a benevolent master, Nell. Are you saying it is not true?"

"The master pretends he is kind and generous. I have never seen him lay a hand on anyone, but he shows up for the beatings or floggings Norris gives to the offender. Jasper intervenes by raising his arms when he feels the punishment is enough. He spouts gospel and forgives the person of their sins. I have watched his face." Nell looked away from Juliet. "He likes it. He feels powerful. And Norris? Aye, he is the devil. He has a whip hanging on a nail by the back door, ready for the next flogging."

"Then why live in his home?"

"I didna ken." Nel shook her head. "'Twas not like this before. The people... Their eyes...The light in them is gone." She placed her head into her hands and wept.

Juliet rubbed her back, waiting for Nell to gain composure. Nell sat straighter and used her handkerchief to dry her eyes and said, "May and I swore we'd never be bound to any person. Norris negotiated with Jasper so we wouldna be servants. He sacrificed himself for us and I was grateful. Jasper added more years to Norris' contract in place of our servitude and had him agree to be the slave master. I assumed it meant he'd oversee these people, assign jobs and made sure the crops were tended and harvested on time. 'Tis not how I thought. Norris barks orders, makes outrageous demands and everyone works from sunrise to sundown even if they are ill. If they do not work or falter for a minute, they feel the crack of the whip."

"How awful." Juliet fought back tears.

"When I lived here before, I performed duties as a maid and was invited to the manor to work. It was such an honor to be asked to clean the Master's study. I dinna ken why I was taken with the man. He gave me compliments and offered sweet treats when he was in the room. Jasper would insist I take tea with him and asked about my life in Scotland. Once he kissed me on the cheek." Nell's hand instinctively went to her face. "I now see him and Norris for what they are. Evil and cruel men."

"What do you plan to do?" Juliet asked. "You sold your house to the Mercers."

"I canna say what I will do or think of the future at this time. I need to care for my bairns. At least I made a friend here so 'tis tolerable. Gwen, the mistress' daughter. Ye ken her?" Nell lifted one corner of her mouth. "What am I saying? Of course, ye do. Yer son is courting her. We all came on the same ship to America."

"Gwen is a kind woman," Juliet said. "I am glad you are friends with her."

"If she and Cowan marry, she will leave, and I will have no one."

"Then do not stay. Come back to Gregor's Cove."

"And do what?" Nell eyes flashed with anger. "Be a maid? A cook? Work for a penny?"

"Nell, I am sorry Angus died."

"'Tis my cross to bear. I never loved him, and 'tis my punishment. The fire took away the only good thing in my life. Angus was kind and gentle. He loved our bairns and would do anything for us. I dinna realize at the time but now I ken it." Nell sniffed and let out a breath. "I also ken what ye were trying to tell me at the Sexton wedding so long ago."

"You do?" Juliet lifted her brows, recalling their conversation.

"You insinuated if I stayed, Jasper would have his way with me. I'd bear his child and be in his service forever. I would have signed a contract for the sake of the bairn." She waved her arm gesturing from one side of the garden to the other. "All this beauty hides the ugliness on this land. Many do the work so few can enjoy." Nell stared out over the landscape and whispered, "I will never get the sound of chains or whips from my mind."

CHAPTER 14

*N*ell's words tore at Juliet's inner core. She'd confided her darkest, most intimate feelings, and Juliet felt unable to help her. Juliet had never been exposed to this lifestyle except what she heard from gossip or Ross. In England, Juliet's family had servants, but none were treated this way, in fact Eva was her best friend. She went on to marry Ross' brother, Duncan. The MacLarens in Scotland had servants, yet those people were considered part of the clan.

"Nell," Juliet said and took her hand. "You were part of the MacDonald clan. The chief's daughter."

"Second daughter," Nell answered in a soft tone. "May…no 'tis the name Norris calls her. I will call her by her given name Mary. Mary's the eldest. Da loved us with all his heart and wanted good matches. Imagine his face when Mary ran off with Norris and married him."

"If I recall, you were supposed to wed a chieftain of another clan."

"The old fool Hugh Munro." Nell pulled at the ribbons of her bonnet and removed it, exposing her beautiful ginger hair piled on her head. "I was to be his son's bride, not his." She made a noise in her throat. "I loved Blair not his Da. Once Hugh laid eyes on me at the Beltane festival, he changed his mind. I was to be his bride, not Blair's.

We planned to run off together and find someone to marry us when we heard the news."

Juliet folded her hands in her lap. *Obviously, they did not run off together. I cannot ask why. Poor thing is so distraught.*

"Do you want to ken why we didna?"

"If you wish to tell me."

"Blair and I set a plan in motion before our families left the festival. We didna want to wait long as Hugh was impatient to marry me. We chose a meeting place and decided to meet the verra next day. On the day I was to leave, one of our stable lads told Da I'd asked him to prepare a horse and have it ready before nightfall. I couldna believe the lad ran off and told my da, but his loyalty was to the clan not me. Instead of meeting my love, Da locked me in my room. He said he loved me but had made a promise. I was to marry Hugh not Blair." Nell covered her face with her hands and took a deep breath.

"Nell, if this is too much…" Juliet gently placed her hand on the woman's arm.

"No." Nell shook her head and dropped her hands into her lap. "If Mary hadna run off with Norris two years before, I think Da would have changed his mind. Mary went against his wishes and he wouldna let it happen again. I never saw him so angry when they returned and announced the news. Then…" Nell looked to the sky. "I had to tell him I was going to have Blair's bairn. He ken Hugh wouldna marry me, and I disgraced the family. By then, Norris had booked passage on the Pembroke, planning to take Mary and their bairn far from Scotland and the MacDonald Clan. Da told me to go with them and never return."

"How awful." Juliet remembered her own sad past, but hers had a happy ending. Nell had yet to find hers. The only piece of Blair the woman had left when she boarded the Pembroke was the baby. It had been born early on the ship, too young to survive, and Norris had tossed the child into the ocean. Juliet shuddered at the memory.

"To this day, Blair doesna ken the reason I didna meet him in the woods. He never kent I would have his bairn." Her voice cracked, and a tear trickled down Nell's cheek. "As I sat in my locked room, I pictured him waiting until sunset, the time we planned to meet. When

I didna come, he stayed hoping something detained me and the moonlight would show me the way."

"Someone must have told him."

"Who?" Nell cried. "Da? I think not." She turned to face Juliet. "I was a foolish lass, Juliet. I let my love for Blair keep me from loving Angus." She inhaled and slowly let the air out. "Perhaps I did love Angus after all. 'Tis too late to tell him. My life has been a series of mistakes." She hung her head. "Thank ye."

"You do not need to thank me, Nell. I did not do much."

"Ye listened." Nell straightened her form, slipped on her black bonnet, tying it under her chin. "We should be heading back to the party," she said in her normal voice. "Craig will hunt me down in the garden if I dinna appear soon."

"A trip to the sweets table may help?" Juliet smiled at Nell. As they walked from the garden, Juliet longed to ask Nell's opinion on her own troublesome thought. All summer Ross debated if he should return with his mother to Scotland and had yet to decide. "Nell, if you could, would you go back?"

"To Scotland?" Nell wrinkled her nose. "Oh, aye. My Blair probably has a wife, but I want to ken. Da may have forgiven me by now. Do ye think?"

"I am sure he has," Juliet answered. She locked eyes with Ross still waiting for her at the table and realized how lucky she was.

———

*R*elieved to see Juliet, Ross met her as the two women strolled towards the table. "I dinna ken how much longer I could stand there without looking like a pig." He chuckled. "How were the gardens?" He offered Juliet his arm.

"Lovely," Juliet answered with a look which told him she had more to tell.

"There you are," Craig called as he approached. He took Nell's hand and put it on top of his forearm. "Jasper invited everyone inside until the heat of the day has passed. Dinner will be served at two o'clock. I would like you to join me, Nell." He nodded at Ross. "My grandson, Jonathan, is quite smitten with your daughter. Perhaps one day he will ask to court her." He gave a slight bow and escorted Nell to a path leading to the house.

Craig's words rendered him speechless. Ross' mouth dropped open as he watched the couple walk to the manor.

"Are the Sextons making matches for their boys today?" Juliet whispered. "They cannot have my daughter. Never."

"Dinna worry, my love. They will have to go through me first." Ross clenched his fists. "We need to get back to Mum. We left her on the porch, promising to bring her something from the table."

"I will get them for you. Go join her." Juliet gave him a nudge.

"Will ye be all right?" Ross brushed a wisp of hair which had escaped her bonnet and tucked it away.

"Of course. I know most everyone here." Juliet lifted her chin. "Look, Glynis and Brodie are gathering the children."

*J*uliet perused the table of fruit pies, peppermint drops, almond cake, cinnamon and ginger biscuits before making her final choices. As she placed the last treat in a linen napkin, a man staggering toward the garden caught her attention. An unfamiliar woman had him by the arm and spoke in a harsh tone. "Milord does not want to see you in a state of inebriation, Norris. Stay in the garden until you get your wits about you."

Norris yanked his arm from the woman's grip. "Off with ye now, Beatrice, and stop with yer high and mighty ways. Ye ken as well as I, Jasper Sexton is no lord. His grandfather bought his way into the gentry class. Call him Master as the rest of us do." He stuck a finger in her face. "But ye and I ken better, dinna we? 'Tis how ye got yer position in the house, curtsying to the family and calling them lord and lady. They gobbled it up and couldna get enough of yer fawning and swooning over them. When we first arrived, ye were no better than any indentured Scot milking cows and tending sheep. Ye practiced yer speech until ye sounded like an Englishwoman, tossing aside yer heritage and loyalty to country." He spit on the ground. "Where is yer bloody pride, woman?"

"Och, Norris, if May could hear you…"

"Dinna speak her name, lass. Ye have no right to say what she would think!"

"It is the drink talking, Norris, so I will forgive you. Yes, I manage the Sexton home and do a fine job. I earned the position. When Lord Jasper asked me to tend to you today, I was more than happy to do so. Now, if you would be so kind to enter the garden, find a bench in the shade and sleep it off!" Beatrice huffed as she grabbed the whiskey bottle from his hand and tossed it in the bushes.

When she marched away, Norris dove into the shrubbery and searched for the bottle. He came up like a man who'd won a wonderful prize, holding the container in the air to examine the contents. Norris looked over his shoulder, and Juliet quickly glanced away, folded the napkin around the sweets and hurried down the path which led to the manor.

"Mum, are ye all right?" Cowan came across the grassy yard to meet her, Gwen on his arm.

"Yes, I am fine. We left your granny on the veranda far too long. I am taking her some sweets and will ask forgiveness." Juliet lifted her hand to show him. The napkin fell open, and she gasped at the sight of crushed cake and biscuit in her palm, not realizing she'd formed a fist around the treats as she walked to the manor. "Oh."

"'Tis all right. We will be eating soon," Cowan said in a kind tone. "Mum, if you please." He offered his arm.

"Thank you," Juliet mumbled. A strange feeling washed over her, and she longed to be with Ross. When she spotted him standing next to his mother's chair, she instantly felt better. She showed him the napkin with the crumbled food and said, "I am sorry."

"Mum is fine. She has been watching the people."

"Aye, Juliet, I enjoy watching the bairns at play. I assume they will have dinner in another room?" Fiona looked up at Juliet and smirked.

Most of the guests had assembled on the veranda while a few stragglers walked toward the house. Two manservants appeared and one announced, "If the women will follow me. I will escort you to the drawing room where you may change and rest before dinner. Gentlemen, Master Sexton has tables for cards set in the back parlor. Please join him after you dress. If you would go with Solomon to the second floor, he will show you the way to your things."

"What about the bairns?" Glynis asked.

"They will be well taken care of," Solomon said with a bow.

"Och, ye and yer fancy ways." Glynis waved a hand. "What if I dinna want to retire to the drawing room?"

"You may stay on the veranda after you dress if you so choose." The man bent at the waist again.

"Sister," Heather said and grabbed her by the arm. "We will go to the drawing room with the others. I want to hear the gossip."

"Ye would," Glynis said with a laugh.

Juliet was familiar with English protocol and it appeared Jasper was determined to impress his guests. They filed into the house, following the women guests to the drawing room. Privacy screens with four silk panels painted with greenery now stood in the corners. Maidservants were situated nearby to help women with their gowns and pack away their day dresses. Heather volunteered to find their trunk of clothes and waved to the others when she found it.

When she finished dressing, Juliet walked with her family from behind the screening into the drawing room filled with the finest of art and tall two-story windows to let in the light. The chair and bench cushions were covered in shades of blue, lilac, silver and gold. The women strolling through the room now wore hooped skirts with layers of petticoats, off-the-shoulder satin dresses with bell sleeves trimmed in lace or ruffles. Juliet had shied away from gold for years because John Alder had favored the color on her. For this occasion, she'd decided to put the past where it belonged and chose a golden fabric with pink embroidered roses.

"I canna decide what chair to sit in, they are all so bonny!" Heather's face flushed with excitement.

"The closest will do, sister." Glynis, wearing a dark green satin with white lace, gestured to a group of chairs. "The place gives me an eerie feeling. The sooner we leave the better."

"But I want to dance after dinner." Heather stuck out her lower lip, smoothing the skirt of her pale blue dress. The silver stripes caught the light every so often and sparkled like jewels.

"One dance. 'Tis all." Glynis narrowed her eyes at her sister.

"Ye feel uneasy because somewhere inside ye ken this could have been yers instead of Sophie's." Heather glared at her.

"Watch yer tongue, lass."

"Heather, Glynis, enough," Fiona said under her breath. "We must present a united front."

"Aye, Mum." Heather hung her head.

"We are MacLaren strong, Mum. Dinna ye worry." Glynis flashed her a grin.

"I ken I have been away for many years, Glynis, but I can see ye still challenge yer sister." Fiona placed her hand on her hips, looking lovely in burgundy.

"Someone has to." Glynis nudged Heather, making her giggle.

"Aye, Mum. Glynis and I are friends now. I never thought we would be." Heather placed her hand on her sister's arm. "Twas a good thing we crossed the ocean together. We wouldna be friends if we never left Scotland."

"I am happy to hear." Fiona dabbed the corners of her eyes with a handkerchief. "Something in my eye." She turned from the group.

"Dinner is served." The announcement quieted the room, only the rustling of dresses could be heard.

The MacLaren women gathered together, walked to the entrance and waited for their men to escort them. Once assembled, the host and his wife would make an appearance and lead the way to the dining hall. After the entourage paraded into the other room, the children would come into the drawing room. Juliet watched the servants scramble to clean up the room while others brought in tables for the children.

Juliet had warned Ross the meal could be long and include at least five dishes for each of the courses before dessert. She chuckled as his eyes lit up at the mention of the food.

The ceremony began with pomp and circumstance. The trio of musicians played while everyone took their seats. Jasper stood with his wife and watched the proceedings, giving a nod to his staff when he saw people were ready.

The first course alone included mushroom broth, beetroot salad, a variety of baked herb-flavored puddings, plain and sweet, a barley-and-raisin dish, stewed beef brisket and bean-and-mushroom casserole. Dinner began when Jasper, as host, served the soup. The guests lifted their wine glasses and toasted each other's health.

"Can we eat now?" Glynis grumbled. "I will never complain about one of our feasts again, Mum."

When the guests finished the first course, the white bone china was whisked away, and clean plates replaced them. Platters of beef, mutton and veal were set in the center of the table. Fish was set at one end, a soup tureen at the other with side dishes, including potato pudding and peach fritters.

After the table was complete, Jasper stood. "Sophie and I want to thank you for coming today and sharing in our celebration." He reached for the carving knife and sliced into the roast beef, cutting several pieces. Once he served those next to him, men began to cut into the meats closest to them, careful not to reach across the table. If something further away was needed, a manservant would be asked to bring it.

The clatter of silverware against china, soft music and the din of voices lulled Juliet almost into a trance. She couldn't believe after ten years, she sat at Jasper Sexton's table once again. The family swore they'd stay away, and they had. Yet, Cowan's eventual marriage would draw them back into their circle.

"Juliet," Ross said, taking her hand. "Are ye all right, lass?"

"Yes, I was thinking of Cowan and Gwen."

"Ye have every right to worry." He squeezed her hand as if he knew what she was thinking.

Desserts of apple cream, cheese, Queen's cake, Bishops' fingers and an assortment of sweet biscuits appeared on the table. Juliet looked toward Glynis and saw the smile on her face. "We have come to the end of dinner," she said to her sister-in-law.

Glynis nodded. "Aye, the best part is finally here."

Port was poured for the gentlemen while the ladies drank sweet wine. After dinner, Sophie stood and said, "I would like to invite the ladies to the veranda and leave the men to drink and converse at the table. Ladies, we need a breath of fresh air after our dinner. The children will also join us."

By the end of August, the sun set earlier in the evening. Once on the veranda, Juliet noticed it had dropped lower in the sky and mingled among the trees, light shining through their leaves. Guests had been invited to stay the night at the Sexton's, but the MacLarens would be in their wagons heading for home when the sun touched the horizon.

An hour had passed before the men filtered onto the back porch to join their wives or chat with friends and acquaintances. Juliet smiled as she watched the young men pair with available girls and knew she'd see them dancing later. Many girls were clustered around Alec and he appeared uncomfortable yet seemed to hold his own. The children played on the grass, not far from where she sat, and her eyes went to Lizbeth. One of the Sexton boys chased her around a bush. *Is he the one who served her tea?* She did not like it, but little she could do.

"Juliet." Ross placed his hand on her shoulder. "We will dance a song or two then prepare to make our leave."

The musicians were setting up on a makeshift wooden floor placed on the grass beyond the veranda. Servants hammered torches into the ground to light the yard when the sun set. When they finished, a lively tune began to play, and the anniversary couple stepped onto the floor. The audience clapped in time to the music while watching the Sextons twirl and spin on the wooden surface. The Sexton boy who'd chased Lizbeth grabbed her hand and joined his parents. The crowd chuckled and encouraged the children's dancing.

Juliet panicked and looked to Ross. She wanted it to stop. He took her hand, glanced over his shoulder at Brodie and Jamie and they followed his lead. Soon the couples were dancing on the wooden floor and more people joined them. Ross spun Juliet toward Lizbeth and her partner, coming to a stop in front of them when the music ended.

Ross bowed. "May I have the next dance, daughter?"

"Why, yes, of course, Father." Lizbeth curtsied, and Juliet breathed a sigh of relief.

As Juliet started to leave, Alec appeared and dipped at the waist. "If I may?" He extended his hand to his mother.

"Thank you, sir." Juliet smiled as she danced with her son. "No one has caught your eye, today?"

"No, I am afraid not. Perhaps I shall wait until I am in Boston?" Alec teased.

When the song ended, the clanging of metal startled the guests. Everyone looked toward the direction of the sound to see Norris Buchanan banging a spoon against a pot. "Hear ye! Hear ye! Gather round, children, for story time!"

Squeals of delight came from the children as parents tried to stop them from running towards the man who could barely stand and was obviously inebriated. Norris rocked from one foot to the other while he waited, pulled a bottle from his pocket and downed a slug of whiskey. "To wet my whistle," he said with a nod. "Now parents, I am not here to harm yer bairns. Step back if ye will. I am only here to claim my own."

A gasp went up in the crowd and they stilled.

"'Tis better. Let me tell ye my tale of woe." Norris used the spoon to point at the people gathered round him. "For those of ye who ken and those who dinna, I had a wife, May Buchanan. She was taken from me in childbirth almost ten years ago." He let out a long and mournful wail. "Oh, May, why did ye have to leave me? She kent I couldna care for two and begged me to fetch her friend to come to our home as she tried to birth the bairn. It lasted two days." He held up his fingers, tears streaming down his cheeks.

Ross charged from the dancefloor, but as he grew close to Norris, three manservants blocked his way. He struggled to push past them, but they held him back.

Norris nodded to the men as if to say they did the right thing. "May had no strength left when our daughter was born and died soon after."

A sympathetic groan went up in the crowd. Norris walked closer to the wooden floor and Juliet clutched Lizbeth, who stood in front of her, by the shoulders.

Norris' voice quivered as he said, "May asked her friend to help me. She kent she would die. Dinna ask me how, but she kent. She wanted her friend to help me through the darkest time of my life. Instead this witch took my child and fled that verra night." He waved the spoon at Juliet. "I tried to get the bairn back but was threatened with my life. I had a son to care for and a job to do." He flung out his arms. "What could a man do? I let this evil woman have my daughter, raise her as her own! My only reminder of May," he cried. "Today I will claim her in front of ye and there will be nothing the MacLarens can do! Come to me, Lizbeth! Ye are my daughter! Elizabeth Buchanan!"

CHAPTER 15

*J*uliet closed her eyes, longing to shut out the world. Norris ranted and raved to the crowd which had gathered closer around him while he shouted of the injustice done to him. Each word he spouted was a lie. He'd given her the child and sent Juliet back to Gregor's Cove without so much as a peek at his daughter. She recalled the scene as if it happened yesterday.

September 1718
Ten years ago

A special message had been sent to the MacLaren home early one morning in late September asking Juliet to come to Sexton Estates. The note said May was in labor and requested her presence.

"I will take ye," Ross said.

"No," Juliet placed her hand on his chest. "It is best if I go alone. If Norris sees you, he might start one of his rants. It will only upset May. Promise me you will stay here?"

"I willna come now, but if ye dinna return by sunset, I canna promise anything."

"Thank you." Juliet took his hand.

"I will get Duchess ready for ye, Juliet." Ross left the house with a frown on his face.

Juliet scoured the kitchen, not knowing what she searched for. Hopefully, they had what was needed at the Buchanan home. She'd never been inside the house but knew the location, down the road from the manor and far enough away not to be seen. She went out the back door to the stables and found Ross standing outside next to her mare. His face said it all. He was angry. She stood on tiptoe and kissed his cheek. "If she does not give birth by nightfall, I will send a message."

"Be careful, my love." Ross swept her into his arms and kissed her gently, the anger dissipating from his face. "I love ye. Dinna let Norris badger ye."

"I will not," Juliet said, and Ross helped her up into the saddle.

The ride went by in a blur as thoughts of May filled her head. Their relationship had been a complex one, ending when May stated she would stay with her husband on the estate. "We offered you a way out, May. I wish you would have taken it, but now I hope you have a good life with your chosen one."

A young barefooted black boy ran from the stables when he saw Juliet approach the house and took hold of the mare's bridle. "Ma'am." He bowed his head.

"Why thank you, kind sir."

His eyes lit up, and he gave her a smile. "I will take good care of her," he said softly.

"I know you will." Juliet refrained from touching his arm or patting his head as she did her own children. Instead, she walked up the path to the front door of the Buchanan home and knocked on the door.

A house slave answered and ushered her inside. "They are upstairs." She gestured toward the steps.

Juliet found May in the master bedroom surrounded by her husband, two more women servants and the town doctor. "Norris?"

Norris looked up, and she saw the pain in his eyes. "Please step outside. I would like to speak with ye."

Juliet went into the hall and waited for him to join her. "Is something wrong?" she asked when he approached.

"She has been like this since yesterday morning. May is losing strength and grows weaker with each passing hour."

"May I ask about Ewan's birth? Was it similar?"

"No." Norris shook his head. "May went twelve hours or so but when the time came, it was quick."

"Why does she need to see me?"

"May wanted to see ye one last time."

Juliet gasped. "She thinks she is going to die?"

"She has a request."

"What?"

"Go in and speak to her but dinna tire her out. If ye do…" Norris grimaced and fisted his hands.

Juliet swept into the room as if she owned the place. "Everyone needs to leave. May wants to speak with me."

The doctor looked at Norris for confirmation. "I will be in the hall if you need me."

Juliet sat on the edge of the bed and took May's hand. "May, I am here. It is Juliet."

May's eyes fluttered open. "Thank the good Lord, ye made it." Her forehead had beads of sweat along the hairline. Her glistening skin was almost as white as the sheets of the bed. "I dinna think I am going to live, Juliet." Tears welled in May's eyes. "I have something to ask ye." Her voice was almost a whisper. "If the bairn is a lass, Norris willna want to raise her if I am gone. I want ye to take her. He already kens what is in my heart."

Juliet inhaled. "No!"

May squeezed her hand. "Ye will give her a good life, Juliet. Ye ken 'tis the right thing. Ye ken the man."

"Well, you are not going to die, May Buchanan. You have had a long, hard labor, and it has taken a toll on you."

"Promise me?" May's eyes locked on to Juliet.

"Only if necessary…and it will not be." Juliet rose from the bed. "I will tell the doctor to come back in. He knows what is best and will help you deliver a strong, healthy baby."

"Ye were a true friend, Juliet. I wasna a verra good one."

"Do not say such words, May. I consider you my dear friend."

"Thank ye." May let go of Juliet's hand.

Juliet left the room and headed straight to where Norris leaned against the wall. "I will take my leave now."

"No." Norris glared at her. "Ye will stay until the bairn is born." He looked at one of his servants who stood nearby. "Take Mrs. MacLaren to the dining room for some tea."

"Yes, Master." The woman gave a slight curtsy.

Juliet followed her down the stairs and into a well-appointed dining room.

"Perhaps you would be more comfortable in the parlor?" The woman waved her hand toward another room.

"Thank you. I believe I would."

Juliet wiled away the hours, looking at books as a distraction and strolled from room to room taking in the décor and looking out windows. Dinner was served at two and the men ate in shifts. She had the doctor for a dining companion for a half hour then Norris took his place. Juliet knew the doctor, and they made idle conversation when not speaking of May. Norris ate in silence, which suited her. She had nothing to say to the man. *How awful he is! I hope he treats the baby well if it is a daughter. I am sure May will protect her.*

As the sun began its descent, Juliet decided it was time to send Ross a message. The baby had not been born, and he'd be on his way to the manor. She rose from the chair to find a servant for paper and pen, startling one of the house slaves as she ran down the stairs and around the banister. She placed her hand on her chest, panting. "Oh! Master Buchanan said to tell you it is done."

"May had the baby?"

The woman nodded. "A girl." She smiled. "With hair like the Mistress."

"And May? How is she?"

The servant dropped her head. "She passed after giving birth as if she knew God's will be done."

"Oh!" Tears pricked the back of Juliet's eyes. "May I go up?"

"Yes, I was coming to get you."

Juliet followed the woman up the steps. The other servant held the baby in her arms, cooing and whispering to the child in a corner of the room. Norris sat on the edge of the mattress, holding May's hand and got up when he saw Juliet. The doctor packed away his bag, shrugged on his coat and passed her as she stopped at the end of the bed.

"Are ye ready to take the bairn?" Norris asked in a business-like tone.

"Please reconsider, Norris. She is your daughter."

Norris lifted a shoulder. "Aye, but I am not fond of wee lasses. Ye spoke with my wife, did ye not?"

"Yes, but I still find it hard to believe…"

"Ye raise my daughter and I keep yer husband's son," Norris snarled. "'Tis a fair trade, dinna ye think?" His face twisted into an evil expression.

Juliet longed to slap him and fought to stay calm, digging her nails into her palms. "Ewan is your son," she hissed.

"Still believing my dead wife's lies?" Norris spit over his shoulder and turned his back on his wife. "I dinna ken why I ever loved the lass."

Despite the vile words coming from him, Juliet could see the hurt in his eyes. He'd loved May since he was a young boy and as much as he wanted to deny it, he loved her still. Norris let his imagination take over, never believing the truth, and ruined his marriage.

Juliet walked to the corner of the room to see the child. She gently touched the orange tufts of hair on the baby's head. "She has May's hair, Norris." She'd hope if he took one look at the child, he'd change his mind.

"What good is a lass?" Norris lifted a shoulder. "She is no use to me."

"Use?" Juliet glared at him.

"As a cook, someone to clean my house? Aye, maybe one day. But I have to waste too many years raising her until she was able."

Indignation rose inside Juliet. If Norris thought the baby was nothing more than a servant, she'd receive no love. "I will take her." She stretched out her arms, and the woman placed the baby in them.

"Good. Be gone with you. Tell Ross I will take good care of his son." His cruel laugh followed her out the door.

Juliet ran from the house, cradling the baby in her arms, never stopping until she entered the barn where the stable boy had taken her horse. Her heart swelled as she looked down at the sleeping babe and whispered, "Elizabeth." The name had come to her the minute she saw her hair. "I will keep you warm, safe and loved."

Her shawl would be the perfect wrap, long and wide enough to put around the baby and bring the child close to her chest. Taking the ends, Juliet draped them over her shoulders and back around under her arms and the baby's body, tying them tightly around her neck.

The stable hand had seen her come in, retrieved Duchess and brought a block of wood to help her mount the horse. "To make it easier, ma'am."

"Thank you," Juliet said to him. Her heart sank every time she visited Sexton Estates and came across a slave, especially one so young. She guessed he was seven or eight. "I appreciate you taking care of her while I was here." She patted his arm.

"It was my honor." He placed his hand over his heart. She took the hand he offered, stepped on the block and carefully lifted her body onto the saddle, keeping one hand on the baby's bottom. The swaddling held and the tiny girl did not stir.

The sun almost touched the horizon as Juliet made her way out to the main road. Her mind raced with ideas of how to care for Elizabeth. Many women in the village would share their milk, someone would volunteer to be a wet nurse, she was positive.

Juliet did not see the rider coming in the opposite direction until he was nearly upon her. "Ross!"

"Juliet! My God, lass! Ye were gone all day. And what do ye have against yer body?"

She felt the baby stir and a loud wail came from Elizabeth. "Your daughter, Ross. I have your daughter in my shawl."

"What? You have a bairn tied in yer shawl?"

As they rode back to the house, Juliet relayed the story.

"Why the bastard…" Ross paused. "No, I willna roll in the dirt with him. We will raise May's daughter as our own and give her a good life."

"It is my first baby, Ross." Juliet's heart fluttered. "I never got to raise Alec from birth, he was three when he came to us."

"The people in the village will help ye, and Glynis' bairn will come in December. She will share her milk."

"Do you think?" Juliet glanced his way.

"I ken so. Ye never looked as bonny as ye do now, with a bairn in yer arms."

"I have already named her, Ross. Elizabeth."

"A bonny name for the bairn with hair like the queen."

"You noticed?"

"Aye." Ross locked eyes with her. "We have to protect Elizabeth from the likes of Norris Buchanan. The less we see of him, the better. We will stay away from Sexton Estates and avoid him in town. When Elizabeth is older, we will tell of the selfish, greedy people who live at the manor and warn her to never go there. The people who have settled on Brodie's land will support us and do as we ask."

"We will never tell her who her father is?" Juliet widened her eyes. "Or about May?"

"I think 'tis best if we dinna." Ross shook his head. "I will make sure everyone kens our wishes."

August 1728—Present Day

$\mathcal{L}$izbeth looked up at Juliet, eyes round as saucers. The fearful expression on her face tore Juliet's heart in two. "Is it true, Mummy? The mean man is my father?"

Juliet dropped to her knees in front of her daughter. "Yes, he is. Oh, my darling dove, we never wanted you to know. Your mother was my friend and asked me to raise you before she died."

"You...are not...my mother?" Tears streamed down Lizbeth's face. She turned to run, but Juliet held her tight. "Let me go!" she screamed.

"Ye heard the lass. Let her come to me, her da." Norris stretched out his arms. "Come to me, my bonny daughter."

"No!" Lizbeth's head turned in one direction then the other, reminding Juliet of a scared rabbit searching for an escape.

Jasper Sexton appeared from nowhere and stepped in front of Norris. "It is time to return the girl to her father. I am sorry it has to be this way, but you should have told her who she was." He pursed his lips and smirked at Juliet. "We will treat her well. My eldest son has taken a liking to the girl, and she will come to the manor with her brother Ewan for lessons. I have acquired a tutor from London who will live here for the school year." He looked over his shoulder. "Take her."

Two slaves came forward, both tall and broad-shouldered. Juliet recognized the stable boy from ten years ago and made eye contact with him. She silently pleaded for him to protect Lizbeth, and he gave a slight nod.

"Yer not so high and mighty now, are ye, Sassenach?" Norris sneered at her. "Be on yer way. Yer not welcome here anymore," he said with a wave of the hand.

Juliet's head spun, and her stomach rolled as she listened to Norris' taunts and her daughter's cries for help as they marched her to the manor. She rushed away from the scene with Ross on her heels. "You should have never made us come here!" she yelled and spun to face him. "What have we done, Ross?"

Her insides wretched and Juliet ran to the bushes. She threw up until she could not stand on her wobbly legs any longer and sank to the ground. Sobbing, she pounded the ground until she had no strength left. Stars danced before her eyes then all she saw was darkness.

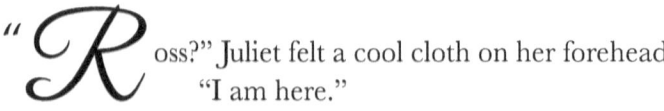

"Ross?" Juliet felt a cool cloth on her forehead. "I am here."

"Lizbeth?"

"I am sorry. We had to leave her at Sexton Estates, Juliet. But it willna be for long."

"You cannot kidnap her, Ross." Juliet struggled to sit up, but his strong hand kept her in place. "They know where we live and will come for her."

"Jasper Sexton and Norris Buchanan will never control us, Juliet. In my heart, I kent I would return to Scotland but couldna admit the truth. We will join Mum on the trip home to Glenhaven. The Pembroke should arrive soon. The day we are to sail, Lizbeth will be on the ship with her brothers."

"Da?"

"Is Cowan here?" Juliet asked, after hearing his voice.

"Aye, he hasna left yer side, lass."

"Cowan." Juliet reached for him and took the cloth from her eyes. "Come, sit. Do you have something to say?"

"Aye, Mum. I plan to marry Gwen and settle in Boston. I dinna wish to go back to Scotland."

"Not even to see your mother?"

"Ye mean my Scottish mum." Cowan hung his head. "I want to see her verra much but…"

"You love Gwen." Juliet paused in thought. "She could come with us."

"I will ask her." Cowan cleared his throat. "Ye dinna think John Alder is looking for me?"

"No, son." Ross placed his hand on Cowan's shoulder. "He doesna ken ye rescued me from prison. He has no proof, even if he suspects. If we return home, we will be safe."

"And remember what Edward told us," Juliet replied. "John married an earl's daughter he met at court last year. They had a daughter. Besides, he lives in England now and has much to do and an estate to run."

"Aye, Mum, I suppose 'tis true. But I would like to finish my studies and become a lawyer. Can I do it in Scotland?"

"I wouldna want it any other way, lad. You can go wherever ye wish to finish your studies," Ross said and smiled at Juliet. "I think we are going home."

"We can only tell your mother, Ross. If word got out…" Juliet pressed her lips together, and a tear rolled down her cheek.

"We tell only the family. I will gather them now." Ross looked to

Cowan. "Will ye gather them?"

"Most are downstairs, Da." Cowan smiled. "They couldna go home while Mum was in such a state. I will make sure everyone is there."

Juliet waited until Cowan left the room. "Ross, are you sure it is safe to go back to Scotland?"

"As safe as it will ever be."

CHAPTER 16

*R*oss counted heads as he strode to the middle of the parlor. Family, young and old, sat or stood in the room, eyes attentive. He checked to make sure Hiram was not among them. If he knew his sister as well as he did, Glynis would have insisted he go to the Gregor home to rest. "The MacLarens have had many dark days," he stated when he came to a stop. "And this has become one of them. We always rise together as a family and will not let it tear us apart. I have come to a decision. One I should have made the day Mum arrived. My family will return to Glenhaven with her."

"What about Lizbeth?" Alec yelled. "Are we leaving her in the hands of Norris Buchanan? She does not deserve that fate." His eyes on fire, Alec stepped forward. "I will stay here to protect her, even if it is from afar."

"Son," Ross said softly. "Do ye think we'd leave yer sister behind?"

Alec brightened. "We are going to rescue her?"

"Aye. Since Cowan is courting Gwen, he has reason to go to the manor. He will get a message to Lizbeth."

"What about Gwen?" Heather asked Cowan. "Will ye leave her or stay in Amboy?"

"I hope she will come to Scotland, Auntie," Cowan answered.

"Oh." Heather looked crestfallen.

"Noah usually stays in port for a few days to visit family," Ross continued. "I hope to convince him to leave as soon as I retrieve my daughter." He glanced at Glynis. "Forgive me?"

"There is nothing to forgive." Glynis met his eyes, and Ross knew what she would say before she spoke. "I am coming with ye, brother. Brodie and I came to an agreement earlier this summer. I will stay the winter and return in the spring. Aaron will come with me, and Rory will stay with Brodie in Gregor's Cove."

"But I am to leave with Uncle Hiram for Boston," Aaron protested.

"Ye can wait a year, son. I want ye to meet yer Scottish family, and yer grandda needs our support."

Aaron hung his head. "I am sorry. Of course, I will go."

"No, dinna be sorry," Glynis said and placed a hand on his arm. "'Tis a lot to ask. But ye get to sail with yer brother, something ye always wanted to do."

Aaron lifted his head and smiled. "You are right. I will be on the Pembroke with Noah."

"Not fair." Rory stomped his foot. "I want to go."

"Ye have to take care of Da for me, Rory." Glynis stroked his cheek.

"Noah promised to bring his monster rifle to hunt the beast in the woods." Rory folded his arms over his chest and huffed.

"Da may have a monster rifle." Glynis looked at Brodie, who Ross thought did not appear happy. Speaking of leaving and Glynis going were two different things.

"Aye, I might," Brodie answered, tousling the boy's hair.

"You do?" Rory dropped his arms. "Why did you not say so?" The boy made everyone laugh, easing the tension in the room.

Fiona rose from her chair and walked to Ross. "I'd hoped you would come home, son." She slipped her arm through his. "Saving Lizbeth is more important. If it doesna happen as ye plan, I want ye to stay here."

Ross fought back tears welling in his eyes. "Thank ye, Mum. I ken ye have grown close to Lizbeth. I swear on our MacLaren emerald I shall rescue my daughter *and* sail to Scotland."

Heather, who'd been speaking with her husband, stepped forward. "I am going, too."

"What?" Fiona covered her mouth with a trembling hand. "I will have all my bairns in Glenhaven?"

"No!" Ross shook his head. "Ye have three bairns to consider."

"Jamie has agreed. People in the village will gladly help until I return. If Da listens to anyone, 'twould be me." Heather looked to Glynis for confirmation.

"'Tis true, Ross, and ye ken it." Glynis nodded. "Heather and I can return to Gregor's Cove together in the spring."

Fiona grasped on to Ross' arm and wept. "I canna believe the strength of my bairns. I would never ask ye to leave yer loved ones, lassies. I only wanted Ross and his family to come home."

Ross bent down and whispered, "'Tis their choice, Mum." He made eye contact with Jamie and Brodie. "Thank ye."

Jamie cleared his throat. "The bairns and I ken she will come home, and I trust yer family, Ross. Now, what can I do to help rescue my niece?"

"I will do anything you want," Brodie added.

"Hopefully, Cowan will speak with Lisbeth at the estate tomorrow. He will let her ken when the Pembroke docks, we will come to rescue her. We'll leave predawn for the manor and have her at the ship by sunrise."

"The rest of us will wait on board," Glynis said. "As soon as I see ye, Ross, I will give word to set sail. I will sit in the crow's nest all night if needed."

"Och, I ken ye would, sister. Thank ye."

"If the messenger was right, the Pembroke should reach Amboy in a day or two. We need to work fast." Glynis scanned the room. "All of us must keep this secret. Go about yer business as if nothing happened at Sexton Estates today."

"I will find and speak with Lizbeth," Cowan said. "Gwen will help me."

"Dinna tell her, son." Ross shook his head.

"I willna, but Gwen had sympathy for Lizbeth after Norris took her away and promised to watch over my sister at the manor. She hasna been treated well by her stepfather and doesna care for Norris Buchanan."

"Bloody hell, every time I hear the name, I wish to strangle the life from him! Norris Buchanan!" Ross ran his hands through his hair and pulled. "The man has been a pain in the arse ever since I laid eyes on him again on the Pembroke."

"Ross," Glynis said. "I think 'tis time for everyone to go to their homes. Hiram went to ours to wait for us. I need to tell him something."

"Tell him a partial truth, Glynis. Ye are going to Scotland to visit family and taking Aaron with ye. He will understand."

"Aye, he will." Glynis turned to her family. "Let us go." When she got to the door, she stopped. "I will pray for Lizbeth, Ross. Please tell Juliet."

"Thank ye, sister." Ross nodded. "Brodie? Let us meet with Jamie at the forgery tomorrow."

After saying his goodbyes to the rest of the family, Ross made for the stairs. In the shadows, he caught sight of his wife sitting on the top step, leaning against the wall. "Ye heard."

"Yes." Juliet wiped under her eyes. "You will rescue my daughter, and we will sail to Scotland. I never thought I would say this, but I am happy to leave."

"Ye dinna mean it, my love." Ross joined her on the step and placed his arm around her back. "'Tis yer home. We will be sad when the time comes."

"Home is where you are, Ross." Juliet leaned her head on his shoulder, and his heart sank as he felt her sorrow.

"Come. Let me put ye to bed. Tomorrow is a new day."

Alec and Cowan had remained in the parlor and together approached the stairs.

"Mum," Cowan said. "I will learn what I can when I visit the manor. My only fear is they won't let me see Lizbeth."

"Cowan!" Rage swept through Ross. In her fragile state, Juliet did not need added stress. He fisted his hands to get control and keep from throttling his son.

"He speaks the truth, Da," Alec said in his brother's defense.

"Mum must be aware it could happen."

"You are right, Alec. I have thought of everything." Juliet covered her eyes with a hand. "Wait!" She looked up at them. "The one slave who took Lizbeth away, I know him. He was the stable boy the day I came to see May. We spoke, and I wished I could do more for him than kind words. He nodded at me as he took her today. Cowan, have you had any contact with a stable hand?"

"Yes, Mum, I believe you are speaking of Gideon."

"He may help us."

"I will remember to speak with him."

Ross helped Juliet to her feet and guided her to their bedroom. He returned to the hallway and called to his sons. They paused in their doorways and walked to him. He grabbed them into an embrace, kissing the sides of their heads, never wanting to let them go.

---

*J*uliet paced the rooms of the house, walked their land and visited the animals throughout the next day, yet time seemed to stand still. She wrung her hands as she strolled toward the front porch, nerves on edge. The sound of a galloping horse caught her attention, and she ran toward the road. "Ross! Come quickly!" she yelled as she passed the barn.

Cowan pulled up his horse at the front gate and jumped to the ground, removing his tricorn hat, exposing his brown hair pulled back in a tail. He tended to his steed as Juliet flew down the path. "Did you see her?" She knew the answer by the look on his face. "You did not."

Ross arrived at her side. "Tell us, son. What did ye learn?"

"Come," Juliet said and slipped her arms through Cowan's. "I have a pitcher of cider on the porch."

Once settled, Cowan rubbed his beard as in thought. "Norris is keeping Lizbeth in the house like a prisoner. She is allowed no fresh air and must ask permission to do anything. During the ride home, I tried to devise a plan to see her."

Juliet wept into her hands. "My poor little dove."

"Mum." Cowan slipped from his chair, crouched in front of her and removed her hands from her face. "I spoke with Gideon."

"You did?" Her heart skipped a beat.

"Aye. He *is* the one ye met ten years ago. He remembers yer kindness."

"Will he help us?"

"He said he will get a message to Lizbeth when he can. There is a rumor she is so despondent Norris may let her go riding with an escort tomorrow."

"Gideon?"

"'Twould be him."

"He could tell her our plan." Juliet sat forward and looked at Ross. "You must pick a place to meet for the rescue. This may be our only chance to get a message to her."

"I will return to Sexton Estates today and speak with Gideon," Cowan said.

"No!" Ross huffed. "Sexton and Buchanan may become suspicious."

"I have reason, Da. I proposed marriage and asked Gwen to come to Scotland with me but swore her to secrecy. I said we wanted to leave quietly for Lizbeth's sake and would return in the spring. I felt bad telling her a lie."

"Ye did the right thing, son." Ross nodded.

"She will give me her answer this evening. I left so she could have time to think." Cowan let out a breath. "I have more news. Remember how Sexton's da kept Nell on his arm at the party?"

"Aye, the old rooster was strutting and crowing like a man half his age," Ross smirked.

"Craig Sexton has asked Nell to marry him before he leaves for England. They will be on the Pembroke when we set sail."

"What?" Juliet shook her head in disbelief.

"He asked her after the anniversary party. Craig and Nell will marry before they depart."

"There is no time for banns to be announced," Ross replied.

"His money will speak for him," Cowan answered.

"And the children? Angus and Sarah?"

"They will go with their mother and Craig." Cowan locked eyes with Juliet. "I believe Gwen will say yes, Mum. She and Nell have bonded as friends. If Gwen kens Nell will be on the Pembroke, 'twill help my cause."

Juliet stayed silent. She wanted to say Gwen should come no matter the circumstances. She needed to love Cowan so much she couldn't live without him. "I wish the best for you, son," Juliet said and touched his cheek.

"We have to put up with the likes of a Sexton on board? I forgot he would be returning to England. Or is he going to Scotland?" Ross asked.

"Craig Sexton does business in Scotland, Da. He spends time in both countries. He may disembark when we reach Crail. 'Tis the reason Nell agreed to marry him, I think. She has never been fond of life in the colonies and gets the chance to return to her homeland."

Juliet lifted a corner of her mouth and shook her head. "No, she has not had the best of times. I hope Craig Sexton is good to her or she may regret her decision."

"In his eyes, Juliet," Ross said. "She is young and beautiful. I hope she is good to him, if ye ken what I mean." He chuckled.

"Ross!" Juliet waved her hand at him then frowned. "There is still one more problem."

"What?"

"Craig Sexton will see Lizbeth on board."

"No, he willna." Ross shook his head.

"Why not?"

"She will be hidden until we are well out to sea. Buchanan can do nothing then. If we need to keep her below deck the entire trip, we will do it. We will wait and see what unfolds after we set sail."

"If you believe it will work, so will I." Juliet stood. "I will leave you men and start supper. Make a good plan to rescue our daughter."

"We will, Mum," Cowan called to her as she let the front door close behind her.

Alone in the house, Juliet swore she heard Lizbeth singing to her dolls. She loved to play school, setting the toys in a row to teach them numbers and letters. When Juliet could, she'd join her daughter and pretend to be the naughty child who would not listen. Lizbeth loved the banter, and they'd laugh until their sides hurt. "Oh, Lizbeth, please forgive your da and me," she whispered.

Juliet placed cheese, bread and leftover stew from dinner on the table and walked to the front door to call the men inside, realizing there were still only two. "Ross, have you seen Alec today?"

"No, I havena. I was asking Cowan the same thing."

"Da!" Cowan gestured toward the road with a nod of the head.

Juliet's gaze went from Cowan to Alec sitting proudly in his saddle with a sword gently swinging from his left hip. He raised his hand in recognition as he trotted up to the front of the house.

"Where have ye been, lad?" Ross called.

Alec dismounted, patted his horse and tied him to the front hitching post. "Uncle Jamie finished the new sword after mine was lost in the fire just in time. We placed the emerald in the handle today. I am ready to rescue Lizbeth!"

"No!" Juliet grasped Ross' arm.

"'Tis a fine idea, son, but ye must escort yer mum to the ship when the time comes. Who will protect her?"

Alec hung his head. "I will, Da, as promised."

He seemed dejected, but Juliet could not bear to see him hurt. "Alec, I will feel safe with you by my side. May I see your sword?"

His eyes shone with pride as he pulled the weapon from its scabbard and held it in the air. "I have used other swords, but this one is truly mine."

"We will go into the woods to practice after supper," Ross said. "Come, yer mum has food on the table."

Juliet noticed Cowan ate quickly and asked to be excused as soon as he finished. Ross gave him permission to leave, and she followed her son to the door. "We will wait up for you. Be careful." She kissed his cheek.

"Do not worry, Mum, I will."

Cowan went out the back door to the stables. Juliet headed to the table but a commotion at the front door stopped her.

"Hey, ho! Anyone home?"

"It is Noah, Ross. He is here!" Juliet rushed to the door to let him in. "Noah! Have you been to see Glynis?"

"Do ya think my mum would have it any other way, Auntie?" Noah hugged her. "I am here to tell ya the crew of the Pembroke is at your service." He bowed. "We will save wee Lizbeth from the clutches of the bloody pig, Norris Buchanan, whether he claims her as his daughter or not."

Juliet's heart soared at the thought "Thank you, Noah. Please come in."

Ross and Alec greeted Noah and immediately began to discuss the rescue plan.

"The best we could leave would be the day after tomorrow, Uncle," Noah said. "It would give ya time to get a message to Lizbeth. We could set sail at dawn or as soon as you are on board."

"'Tis all I ask, Noah."

"So much has happened since I left." Noah rubbed his face. "I cannot believe I am taking the family back to Scotland. Mum, Aaron, Aunt Heather and all of your family."

"Dinna forget my mum." Ross chuckled.

"Miguel would have my head if I did." Noah smiled.

"Does he still pine for my mother?" Ross asked in a harsh tone.

Noah's smile disappeared. "We have not spoken of her, Uncle. But I know he cares. They became friends."

"Make sure it stays that way." Ross folded his arms over his chest.

"Ross! Let us not worry about Fiona and focus on Lizbeth. Noah, we appreciate what you are doing."

"Ya do not have to thank me, Auntie. We are family."

"The family is growing, Noah," Ross said. "Cowan has asked Gwen to marry him. He went to Sexton Estates to get his answer tonight. There might be one more passenger on board."

"Beside Nell and her two children? Mum did not tell me Cowan and Gwen were close to marriage, but we will find room for her." Noah replied. "Craig Sexton sent word he'd bring three more passengers and wanted another cabin, but I have one or two more available."

"Does it seem odd?" Juliet looked at them. "So many of us came here over the years, and now, we return to Scotland as a group?"

"Aye, ye are right, wife. We have been neighbors, friend or foe, yet we have one thing in common. The Pembroke."

"I hope it brings us together," Noah said. "And if not, it is a long trip with nowhere to go but the sea."

Ross laughed. "Verra true, lad." He turned to Juliet. "Now we wait for our son to come home with good news."

CHAPTER 17

*T*he MacLarens gathered at Ross' home the next day. Glynis had not seen the family this serious since the day she left Scotland with Heather and Jamie twelve years ago. Her eyes burned from little sleep, but it was worth feeling tired. She'd stayed up most of the night making love to Brodie, breathing him in one last time before they parted. Her love grew deeper each year, and she didn't think parting would be this hard. In the dark of the night, they'd cried in each other's arms then did not speak of it again.

Glynis had packed a trunk for her and Aaron, letting Noah take it to the ship. Rory would join her later at the Pembroke, and she'd let him climb to the crow's nest to keep watch. Brodie would retrieve him at dawn when he arrived with Ross and the others. *If they are successful.* She hated the feeling of dread that overcame her and prayed their rescue plan worked.

Noah had sent crew members throughout the town and to Sexton Manor, informing people they must board the ship tonight if they'd booked passage to England. The men were ordered to help passengers achieve the goal in any way they could and escort them to the ship if needed. Miguel insisted on escorting Fiona saying she needed protection. Her mother appeared flattered, and Glynis had to stop Ross from interfering.

Beside Brodie, Glynis's other regret was leaving her good friend, Hiram Coward. Her mind drifted to yesterday morning, the day he left for New York. She'd asked him if they could speak alone before his departure and they'd risen before dawn. It was just the two of them in the kitchen where they settled in for their talk. Glynis prepared tea and porridge, wanting to make sure he had food in his stomach for the journey. As she worked, she told Hiram about the trip and how her son and nephews would join them on the voyage to Scotland. He had been disappointed to hear Aaron and Alec would not return to Boston with him but understood.

"I trust ye, Hiram, and ye must tell no one." Glynis had said to him. "Lizbeth will be rescued."

Hiram, also a guest at the anniversary party, had witnessed the scene. He'd held up his hands to stop her and said, "Tell me no more."

"I will respect yer wishes."

Hiram then approached her, placed his hands on her shoulders and said, "I would like to ask you something. I, too, would like it to stay between us."

"Ask me anything."

"I would like to kiss you... Just once, if I may." His eyes filled with tears. "I am afraid I will never see you again and would like a remembrance of our friendship."

Glynis mulled the request over in her mind. *What harm can it do? We are friends.* She saw the sadness in his eyes. He'd loved her all these years, and she could never return his feelings. Her heart tore in two, and tears pricked the back of her eyes. She did love him. Not in the way he wished, but she did. "Ye may."

Hiram's lips found hers and he gave her a soft and gentle kiss. She'd hugged him goodbye, feeling his body shudder underneath her hands. They stood locked together while he quietly wept and Glynis rubbed his back like she did her children when they were sad.

A gust of sadness and regret swept through her. Glynis fought back the tears which welled in her eyes as she recalled their years together. Whatever the situation, good or bad, Hiram stayed true to her.

Determined to do something for him, she planned to send a note to Edward, begging him to reconsider Hiram's offer. It was the least she could do. "I will see ye again," she had whispered in Hiram's ear as a tear trickled down her cheek.

Glynis' heart wretched at the thought of leaving the place she'd begun to call home. At one time, she would have given anything to sail the world and make new discoveries. Her wanderlust days were behind her and her skills as a hunter and provider had taken its place in recent years.

"You are so still, sister," Heather said. "If I didna ken yer breathing, I would check to see if yer dead."

Glynis could tell her sister joked from nerves and was worried about the family she'd leave in Gregor's Cove. "I never saw a dead body stand straight up, lassie." She wrapped her arm about Heather and tugged her closer. "I was thinking, 'twas all. So much has happened this summer. Did ye ever think we would go home to Glenhaven?"

"I thought of it often but felt it a dream."

"Well, now we go. Da will be surprised. Eh?"

"Aye, I long to see him, Glynis, but my heart is torn and hurts so badly."

"We will be back here standing in this verra spot next year. 'Tis only ten months away."

"Sounds like a lifetime."

"Och, we will laugh about it next year." Glynis rubbed her sister's arm. "Did ye hear the good news? Gwen said yes to Cowan's proposal and will sail with us to Scotland."

"Will they marry in Glenhaven? There is no time to do it properly here." Heather lifted her brows. "We can help, Glynis. I am verra good at weddings."

"Ye are." Glynis recalled her wedding to Brodie in Heather's backyard. Her sister made sure everything was perfect.

"Heather? Glynis?" Fiona called to them. "I am leaving now and will see you on the Pembroke." She gathered them in her arms. "Pray for Lizbeth," she whispered. "I have trust in Ross and yer husbands but 'tis the others I dinna. I only met the Sextons once, but…" She shook her head.

Ross appeared agitated as they watched Miguel help Fiona into the wagon. Glynis glanced around the yard and spotted her son. "Aaron, go with yer granny. I will join ye at the ship."

"Yes, Mum." Aaron hugged Brodie one more time and ran to the wagon.

Fiona held out her arms to him. "Oh, my blue-eyed bonny lad. Come."

"I hope that helps, Ross," Glynis said under her breath, and all he did was grunt in response.

Glynis chose not to go to battle with Ross over Fiona and Miguel's friendship now. He had much on his mind and did not need to banter with his sister at this time. The men had agreed when the sun reached the horizon, the women would head for the ship, leaving Ross, Jamie and Brodie at the house. Noah had the crew ready to sail at first light. All they needed was Lizbeth to complete the family.

*J*uliet was the last to board the Pembroke. She'd sent Alec ahead to find their cabin and arrange for their trunk to be delivered to the right one. The family embarked at different intervals, hopefully to go unnoticed. A group of women climbing the gangway without their men may draw attention. If anyone approached Juliet or asked her questions when she boarded, she had answers ready.

Noah had instructed his crew to make sure the passengers were below deck at sunset and order them not to come up top until sunrise. Not his usual rules, some who'd sailed with him before grumbled at the request, but Juliet hoped they obeyed. As she climbed the gangway, she noticed a lone figure standing at the bow of the ship, gazing over the town of Perth Amboy.

Juliet pulled her shawl around her shoulders and headed for the woman dressed in black. "Nell?"

"Aye?" Nell turned her head, and Juliet saw Lizbeth's beautiful cornflower blue eyes staring back at her. "Oh, 'tis you, Juliet. Ross has made his decision? You are returning to Scotland."

"Yes, we are going to Glenhaven to check on his father and return in the spring," she lied.

"I didna see him board with ye." Nell tilted her head to see around Juliet.

"Have you been on deck long?" Juliet asked hoping to distract her.

"No, I came up for air before we are sequestered for the night. The crew is patrolling the halls as if we are common criminals." The corners of her mouth twitched.

"Ross has taken his mother to her cabin. I am to wait for him, and we will go to ours, hopefully before the sun sets. I do not want to break the rules." Juliet forced a laugh.

"I think Noah would allow you privileges the rest of us willna have."

"I doubt it. He is a strict captain." Juliet tried to keep the conversation light and hoped Nell didn't have too many prying questions.

"It must be hard to leave Elizabeth behind. You will not see her for months."

Juliet's heart skipped a beat, and she flinched at the statement. Trying her best to give a positive outlook, Nell now reminded her of the worst-case scenario. If Ross did not rescue her, Lizbeth stayed in America while they sailed to Scotland never to see her again. She walked to the railing where Nell stood and gazed out over the town. "Yes," she whispered. "Having a child ripped from your arms is torture." She turned and locked eyes with the woman. "I do not have to explain to you, do I?"

"No, ye dinna. My lassies are in heaven with their Da. 'Tis the only thing that keeps me sane, thinking of them playing on the clouds singing and laughing." Nell placed her hand on Juliet's. "I saw my niece before I left. I told her I was Mary's sister, her Aunt Nell. She was kind and sweet, Juliet. Lizbeth hugged me and wished me well when I told her I was leaving with Craig."

"Thank you for sharing, Nell. Lizbeth was doing well?"

"Aye, she looked as if she'd cried for days but is trying to be brave."

"I heard you wed Craig Sexton. Best wishes on your marriage."

Nell's nostrils flared. "I didna marry the man yet." She squeezed Juliet's hand which she still held. "I am sorry. I dinna mean to sound angry at ye." She let out a breath. "Ye seem to come along when I need to speak about my problems."

"There is a problem?" Juliet lifted a brow.

"I told Craig I wanted to wed in front of the MacDonald clan and have my father give me away. I used every womanly charm I had to convince him to wait. He is a proud man and when I said I wanted to show my people I was marrying an Englishman of stature. He granted my wish. We have separate cabins, one for him and one for me and my bairns."

"I can understand your wish to wait. Things happened quickly."

"I will never marry the bloody bastard." Nell lifted her chin defiantly in the air.

What? "Nell, you are a widow with two children. What will you do?"

"Once I return home, I will ask Da for help. If he canna or willna, I will return to Crail and live with Angus' family. Aggie has written many letters over the years. She will take us in. I plan to speak with her before we set off for my homeland. I refuse to be in a loveless marriage, bound to a person for life and an old Englishman at that. I couldna marry Hugh Munro and I canna bear the thought of sleeping next to Craig Sexton."

Again, Juliet did not know how to answer or if she condoned the idea, but she gave the woman credit and thought her plan might work. "You are welcome at Glenhaven if it does not go as you want. I will make sure you are treated properly, as a laird's daughter."

Nell smiled. "So no cooking or cleaning?"

"No." Juliet shook her head. "I wish you the best and will help in any way I can."

"I may need your help. Craig is trying to convince me to wed on board the ship, and ye ken the reason why." Nell pressed her lips together and folded her arms. "I said we wouldna share a bed until we marry. He promises to take me to the MacDonalds when we land, but I dinna trust him, especially if we marry."

"Does Craig have business in Crail? Do you plan to disembark there or continue to London?"

"Craig promises we will get off in Crail. And if he doesna? I will gather my bairns and leave the ship without him."

---

*T*hree men stepped out into the dark skies of the early morning. Ross recalled what Glynis had taught him from his time on the ship. Dawn came in three stages. Signs of light in the dark sky would come first. The countryside would appear gray, but they'd be able to see. When bright colors of pink or gold appeared along the horizon, the second stage of daybreak had begun. Ross wanted to be on his way to the ship by that time, knowing the sun would soon follow and rise in its full glory to announce the start of a new day. They walked in silence to the barn to prepare the horses for the journey to the manor. Each man carried a lantern which would be extinguished as soon as they could see their way without them.

The men rode until they were a quarter mile of the estate. They tied the horses to branches along the side of the path as Ross and Jamie planned to finish on foot, leaving Brodie with the animals. The soles of their feet made a crunching sound as they walked toward their destination. The split rail fence signaled they had arrived at the edge of the estate where Lizbeth was to wait at its farthest corner.

Ross' heart pounded against his chest and he held his breath as he studied his surroundings. Jamie made hand gestures as if he saw something. Ross squinted into the predawn light and made out two shapes on the other side of the fencing. He nodded at Jamie to proceed and followed.

"Da!" A voice whispered.

Ross rushed to the railing, tears filling his eyes. "Lizbeth!" The sky had grown lighter and everything appeared gray. He looked toward Gideon and extended his hand. "Thank ye, lad."

"No need to thank me, Master MacLaren. Lizbeth did not deserve this fate."

"And neither do you," Ross answered. "Come with us."

Gideon hung his head. "I cannot."

"Why? Ye are held against yer will and receive no pay."

"Others will suffer if I leave."

Verra clever, Sexton. "I am sorry to hear. I dinna like to leave ye behind, Gideon."

"I like the horses and the stables, sir. Many work in the hot sun all day. so, my job is not as bad."

Ross noticed a horse tied to a tree. "Ye brought Lizbeth here?"

"Yes, and I must warn you I will have to report the horse missing when I return." Gideon smiled. "But it takes a while to walk back to the stables on foot."

"'Tis all the time we need. Be careful, Gideon. Blame us if the need arises."

"I will not have the need. My mother oversees Master Buchanan's home. She will discover Lizbeth missing from her bed when she goes to wake her." Gideon turned to leave and paused. "Tell Mistress MacLaren I always appreciated her kindness."

"I will."

"Gideon, wait!" Lizbeth beckoned to him. She threw her arms around his neck and said, "Thank you."

"May the Lord be with you." Gideon pulled away and his hand went to his cheek, brushing something from it.

They watched him walk into the shadow of the trees then Lizbeth climbed onto the fence. Ross scooped her into his arms and ran, not stopping until he reached Brodie and the horses. She buried her head in his shoulder to muffle her cries, and Ross had to hold back the anger he felt for Norris. Protecting his little girl became his number one priority.

Lizbeth still wore the same dress from the party and had no shawl to protect her from the morning chill. He grabbed a blanket from his saddle bag and wrapped it around her. "Ye are being a good lass. Dinna speak until we are far away," he whispered.

The sound of the horses' hooves pounded in Ross' ears as they galloped toward the town. His sense of hearing was on high alert, listening for any noise behind them. When they reached the edge of Perth Amboy, he let out a sigh of relief.

"Where are we going, Da?" Lizbeth spoke her first words since liberation.

"To the Pembroke and on to Scotland. We are going home."

---

*G*lynis detected three horses in the distance and nudged Rory who'd fallen asleep. "They are coming, son. Get on yer feet."

The colors of the morning filled the sky, and she watched in awe at the glorious sight. "God is smiling on ye, Ross."

"What did you say, Mum?" Rory rubbed his eyes.

"Time to climb down. Are ye ready?" She swung her leg over the basket and helped him do the same. "Hold tight."

Glynis stayed below him, guiding his hand and foot movements. When they reached the deck, she twirled him in the air. "Remember this time together with yer mum, Rory. Keep it in yer heart until the next time I see ye."

Rory threw his arms around her waist. "I do not want you to leave, Mummy." He sobbed into her shirt.

"I will be back, son, I promise." Glynis petted his head. "Come, we need to tell yer auntie her daughter is here." *But do I ken for sure she is with the men? I didna see the lass.*

After the family gathered on deck, staying quiet so other passengers would not hear, Glynis ran down the gangway to greet the men. As soon as she spotted Lizbeth, she let out the breath she held. "My bonny niece, yer safe. Praise God." She took her from Ross, hugged her close and whispered. "Ye must stay silent. No one can ken yer here."

Brodie slipped from his horse, Glynis put Lizbeth on the ground and rushed to him. "Be safe," he said.

"I will." She pressed her lips against his. "I love ye, Broden Gregor."

"And, I love ye, Glynis Gregor." Brodie turned to Ross. "I could not put her in any safer hands. Go with God."

The men embraced, and Brodie backed away. "I will stay on the dock until I cannot see you, Glynis."

"And I will be at the stern of the ship to do the same."

165

Heather had run down the gangway and was in Jamie's arms. He released her and looked at Glynis and said, "I ken ye will…"

Glynis held up her hand. "Ye dinna have to say it, brother. I will take care of her."

---

*R*oss waited until the family had said their goodbyes on the docks. He stared up at the ship's deck where Juliet waited, hand on her heart. He lifted his, signaling he was coming aboard with their daughter. "Glynis? Heather? 'Tis time."

One last kiss was shared between husband and wife, tearing Ross' heart in two. Guilt consumed him even though he knew they'd chosen their fate. Much could happen during the crossing, he'd seen a storm take four lives. No one knew what waited for them in Scotland, and he prayed their return would not change things for the people of Glenhaven. "To the unknown," he whispered.

The family gathered together and walked as one to the ship. They passed Rory on the gangway as he ran to join his father. "Be good, lad," Ross said as the boy threw his arms around him.

"I will, Uncle." The boy looked up at him with such love. "I hope to see you again."

Ross could make no promises but answered, "I hope so, too."

"Lizbeth!" Rory hugged her next. "You are free."

"I am, Rory. I will miss you. Be a good boy for your da."

"I will try." Rory smiled.

"If you will excuse me, there is someone I need to see." Lizbeth returned his smile.

Lizbeth broke free of her father's hand and ran the rest of the way to the deck of the ship, her golden copper locks flying in every direction, until she reached Juliet.

"Mummy! Mummy!" She raced into her mother's arms, sobbing and laughing. "Norris Buchanan is a horrible man," she said. "I dinna care if he says he is my father. He only wanted me to live there because Jonathan Sexton liked me. He said to be extra kind to him, and he'd marry me one day." She turned to Ross who'd followed her up the ramp and wrapped her arms around his waist. "You are my Da. My only true Da."

Alec and Cowan joined them, arms extended around the family, drawing them into a circle. Ross fought to hold back tears and the emotions he'd kept in check. He looked at Juliet over the top of Lizbeth's head. "We have our family together." He searched for Glynis. "Shall we set sail?"

"Aye, Ross, I will tell Noah 'tis time."

"But first?" Ross motioned for the others to assemble around his family group. "Remember no matter where we are or where we go, we are MacLaren strong."

"MacLaren strong," they whispered in unison as the sun made its appearance on the horizon.

CHAPTER 18

*H*e hid among the trees where he could not be seen near the shores of the Raritan River. For a younger man, his hair had turned prematurely gray. The unkempt salt and pepper beard hung to the top of his worn breeches. He tugged the wool coat closer to his body to fight off the chill of the damp morning air but refused to leave until he saw the ship.

The Pembroke finally came into view, tall and proud. It majestically sailed from the Perth Amboy port toward the Atlantic Ocean. Mesmerized, he watched the vessel glide across the bay. He stepped from the shadows of the forest, edging closer to the water's edge, straining to see the last of the ship before it reached the sea. One lone figure stood at the far edge of the stern, hand in the air, as if to say goodbye to the town.

"God speed," he whispered.

When the Pembroke disappeared from his sight, tears welled in the man's brilliant blue eyes. He turned from the mouth of the Raritan River and faded into the woods as quietly as he had come.

THE END

ACKNOWLEDGMENTS

Every time I enter the MacLaren World, I am whisked away to another time and place. I try to picture living in the 18th century and what it would be like. They, of course, did not have amenities we have today, yet what ties us together throughout the years is the same. Love, friendship, sacrifice, tragedy and so many other emotions and events are woven into the fabric of all our lives.

Ross, the chief of the clan in America, has been placed into a position many have experienced. Where do your loyalties lie? Family or Country? Yet, he carries a bigger burden. Responsibility. Ross is next in line to be Laird of Glenhaven back in Scotland.

I hope you enjoy the MacLarens as much as I love writing about them. I may have to make a family tree to keep up with them. Through births, adoptions, guardianships and marriages they keep growing.

I want to thank my publisher, Nancy Schumacher, for supporting the series. What started out as a short story grew into this saga of the MacLarens. She deserves more than a few lines in an acknowledgment with all she does for her authors at Melange Books. So thank you, Nancy.

Chris Hall. What can I say? My editor is wonderful, marvelous and all around great! Thanks go to her for all her help and support.

Cover artist, Caroline Andrus, did it again! Awesome as always.

Also, thanks to family and friends who read and support this series.

Finally, a big thanks to my husband, Ron, who is proud of every book I write.

ABOUT THE AUTHOR

After a great career in teaching, Nancy found a second calling as a writer. Born and raised in Northeast Ohio, she currently resides in Mentor, OH. Ohio is her home, but she loves to travel the U.S. Now Scotland is on her bucket list as a place she'd like to visit. Nancy is married and has one son.

www.nancypennick.com
www.facebook.com/nancypennickauthor

ALSO BY NANCY PENNICK

With Satin Romance

The Clan MacLaren Series

My Highlander Husband

Donnach's Daughter

The Heart of the Emerald

Now and Forever

Featured in the Following Anthologies

Frozen Moments in Frozen

The Perfect Beginning in Second Chance for Love

Chili Warmed Her Heart in Food & Romance Go Together, Vol 2

With Fire & Ice Young Adult Books

Waiting for Dusk Series

Waiting for Dusk

Call of the Canyon

Stealing Time

Taking Chances (Free!)

Broken Dreams

Second Chances

www.ingramcontent.com/pod-product-compliance
Lightning Source LLC
Chambersburg PA
CBHW020128180626
46810CB00004B/1451